T0157191

MAD DOG STEEL TIME

By Dennis Perry

iUniverse, Inc.
New York   Bloomington

Mad Dog Steel Time

iUniverse books may be ordered through booksellers or by contacting:

iUniverse
1663 Liberty Drive
Bloomington, IN 47403
www.iuniverse.com
1-800-Authors (1-800-288-4677)

Because of the dynamic nature of the Internet, any Web addresses or links contained in this book may have changed since publication and may no longer be valid. The views expressed in this work are solely those of the author and do not necessarily reflect the views of the publisher, and the publisher hereby disclaims any responsibility for them.

ISBN: 978-1-4502-1930-3 (sc)
ISBN: 978-1-4502-1931-0 (ebook)

Printed in the United States of America

iUniverse rev. date: 6/4/2010

Cover by Diane Olsen

Dedicated

To the hard working line hands who get electricity where it's
supposed to go.

ACKNOWLEDGMENT

This book couldn't exist without the help and encouragement of Everett 'Mad Dog' Perry, a professional lineman. His explanation of line work on steel towers is the glue that holds *Mad Dog Steel Time* together. And, as he puts it, "the rest is fiction."

Other books by Dennis Perry

Fiction
Adult Books
Missing in Paradise
The Copper Thieves

Young Adult
Yakabou Must Choose

Children's Books
Achoo!
Sunny and the Dragon

CHAPTER 1

The funeral director had to borrow folding chairs from the American Legion to accommodate the final viewing of Clayton Wilson's body. The funeral director wasn't surprised. Everyone in town wanted to take a last look at an old friend, and some wanted to make sure Clayton was really dead. The former greatly outnumbered the latter.

Filer Wilson, Clayton's only offspring, was working at the top of a power pole when a Portland police vehicle pulled up beside the P.G. & E. service truck at the bottom of the pole. Filer looked down at the police car and thought, "There's bad news for someone." An hour later he pulled into his driveway in Albany, Oregon. He hurried to enter the split level home he and Abbey, his wife, now owned. Abbey and Kylie, his eighteen year old adopted daughter, were waiting for him in the kitchen.

This was the first time Abbey had seen her husband stunned and without anything to say. Usually he made a comment that put the family at ease. Abbey realized it was up to her to be the strong one now, helping Filer until he could think about other things rather than his loss.

"Maggie called," Abbey said.

Abbey had been a member of the Wilson family long enough to know of the unusually strong bond between Filer and Clayton.

"I told Maggie we'd leave here when you got home from work. We're packed. There's a bag on our bed with underwear in it, you just need to put in whatever else you want for the funeral."

After Filer had a few words with Maggie on the telephone, the Filer Wilson family loaded into Abbey's four door sedan. Abbey took the driver's side with Kylie riding shotgun. Filer arranged a pillow against the door behind Abbey and fell asleep. If he woke up during the six hour drive he didn't say anything. Abbey and Kylie spoke little and in whispers. The drive they were making had been a happy one for them in the past; now they felt Filer's grief. Clayton and Maggie Wilson had also become an important part of their lives.

With sorrow and grieving at the end of their journey it ended too quickly. Abbey parked on a side street a little way from the Wilson home. Parking beside the home was already taken.

Inside his childhood home family and friends had gathered to be with Maggie. Clayton's brother Paul and his wife Ellen greeted Filer at the back door. Maggie was where she felt the most comfortable, in the kitchen. Friends from her card club were seated around the kitchen counter reminiscing of the times the card club met in her home with Clayton happily escaping to go drinking at Stoney's.

Maggie pulled Abbey and Kylie into her arms when they entered the kitchen. After a hug she introduced them to her club members. Filer put his arm around her shoulders and sighed when he felt her distress.

Vera, president of the card club, got a casserole out of the fridge and put it in the oven to warm up. Soon she served the travelers a dinner of leftovers. Maggie sat with them and talked quietly. The rest of the card club moved to the living room where some sat for a while and others said good-bye and left. They were good friends and would be back the next day to support Maggie.

"He died suddenly of an aneurysm. We were watching T.V. and he leaned forward in his easy chair, then he was gone. The railroad doctor came and tried to revive him but he was gone," Maggie sat back on the sofa and rested.

The ritual of who slept where distracted Filer from thoughts of Clayton. Members of the extended Wilson family found rooms with beds for the night and the household quieted.

Filer lay with Abbey and drifted off to sleep. In a dream, a rare event for Filer, Clayton touched him on the shoulder, and when Filer opened his eyes the old man was there again, like the many times before when he wanted Filer to go on some wild adventure with him. "Sorry Filer,"

Clayton said, "I had to go on this one alone." Before Filer could grasp what was happening, Clayton disappeared.

Filer woke up alone in bed. He got up, showered and dressed. Fragments of the previous night's dream came back to him as he walked upstairs into the kitchen. Women of the Wilson family, including Abbey and Kylie, were helping Maggie cook breakfast. Filer sat down beside Paul.

"The good ones die young," Paul commented.

"What?" Filer asked.

"The old saying about the good dying young applies here; Clayton was a young man."

"I'm not so sure about the good part," Filer said, "but I think the old man lived every minute of his life."

"I agree," Paul said, "Clayton enjoyed living more than most people."

Their conversation continued with stories of Clayton getting them involved in various adventures.

When the meal was finished Maggie asked Filer's and Paul's advice for the funeral services. It was a courtesy because she had already made final plans for Clayton.

On the hour of the final viewing, Filer sat with Abbey and Kylie on his right side and Maggie on his left. It was on him now. Clayton's death had been unexpected and it kept coming back to him to think there wouldn't be any more July 4th picnics or Christmas Eves with the old man. Clayton had been his rock, if an unpredictable rock.

Filer watched Homer Swift as he stood respectfully at the open casket with his stripped railroad cap in his hand.

Filer didn't find it unusual that a middle-aged townie called Earl, Clayton's and Homer's nemesis, also sat in the audience waiting for the eulogy to get started. Others might think it a little strange that Earl was at the memorial after the long ago altercation at Stoney's.

In his later years, Clayton was shorter that Filer, but with a life time of physical activity, Clayton had a solid muscular build. Now without a spark of life in the body he left behind, family and friends felt emptiness where life had once leapt out of Clayton to animate a mostly positive reaction in them.

Clayton had woken Filer one evening and hurried him to Stoney's to protect Homer from Earl. It had been a game of keep away involving Homer's stripped railroad cap, more suited to children on a playground than to adults. Filer tried reasoning with Earl, and when Earl took a swing at Filer, Filer laid him out. Now both of these men were here paying their respects.

A member of the local Masonic Lodge stood up and walked to a podium on the dais behind the casket. He got the eulogizing under way and after he completed his fifteen minutes in front of the crowd he turned the podium over to an American Legion veteran. It was mentioned that Clayton served his country; was always willing to help out when called on, and that he was a good drinking companion. One of Clayton's oldest friends stood up and declared Clayton to be a good cowboy in his day. If he hadn't tired of the cowboy life he might have won a national championship. When that old friend left the podium, the Masonic officer came forward again and offered the podium to anyone else in the hall who wanted to say a few words. Before he stepped away from the podium he looked at Filer, indicating the podium was his if he wanted it.

Filer glanced at Maggie and she gave a slight nod. Then he felt Abbey squeeze his arm, a gesture to give him courage with whatever he decided. Filer stood up slowly, carrying as great a weight as any time he'd ever climbed a sixty foot pole wearing a full utility belt, and walked to the front of the crowd of mourners. He didn't have the slightest idea of what he would say until he was a few steps from the podium. Then it came to him as he squared himself behind the podium.

The gathering waited politely, but apprehensively for the tall, bearded man to say his words.

"I want to thank everyone for their sympathy and kind words for Clayton Wilson." Filer paused for a moment gathering his thoughts. He gripped the podium as tightly as a lineman hanging onto the top of a pole in a high wind, and said, "I could tell you stories about Clayton. And a lot of you would be in those stories, but we can save the stories for later. Right now all I want to tell you is that Clayton's death came as a surprise. It's like the times he woke me up in the middle of the night to say we had some situation to take care of," Filer found Homer in the audience and smiled at him, "now Clayton has gone for an adventure without asking me to help him out." Filer looked down at his family and gathered strength. "I hope he's got his situation under control where ever his spirit is, and is smiling at what he's heard this afternoon."

Filer made himself release the podium and looked for the Masonic officer as he walked back to his seat to be with his family. He'd told a lot of bar room stories to linemen, some were winners and some weren't, but none of them had affected him like this short eulogy for a man he'd continue to miss for the rest of his life. He was glad when he sat down to have Abbey take one arm and Maggie the other.

CHAPTER 2

Shane McLane parked his older model Ford pickup beside his partially constructed mountain cabin. With the success of his latest action picture, and a contract signed for a sequel, he'd upgraded the original A-frame plans to a three thousand square foot custom made log cabin.

Shane wanted a comfortable place away from Hollywood to spend time between pictures. In the nearby town of Deer Lodge wearing sunglasses and a Caterpillar baseball cap he could walk the small Montana town without being recognized.

At the cabin site Shane looked over the cabin plans with his General Contractor Dave Walker.

"We're giving you an emergency generator in case of problems with the local power company. They're very reliable, but snow loads get heavy and it's possible your power could be knocked out."

"That sounds like a good plan. I don't know how much time I'll be spending here during the winter, but it's better to be safe than sorry."

"One thing, Shane, the local power company has a six month backlog on building power lines to these forest sites. I recommend hiring a private outfit to build your power line. It'll cost you an extra five thousand dollars," Dave gave Shane his opinion; "It'll be well worth it if you want local power when you move in."

"What's an extra five thousand, huh? Hopefully by then my agent will have me an advance on another picture. I'm hot now, you know."

"Great, so you want me to find a local outfit to do the power line?" Dave let a small smile breakout. He'd just been given the go ahead to make a little extra money on this job. He felt a little bad because he liked Shane McLane better than he liked his pictures.

Dave decided he'd try his luck finding local help for building the private power line at the Broken Arrow bar in Deer Lodge.

CHAPTER 3

Ozzie Harper came into the Broken Arrow and sat at the bar. Ozzie was a little taller than average. He wore a soft brown suede leather vest over a white dress shirt tucked into ironed Levis. He replaced his heavy work boots with comfortable cowboy boots. Anyone forming a first opinion of Ozzie's character at first glance, would judge him to be a confident, outgoing individual.

As usual the Arrow was filling up even before the band started playing. Dave Walker was seated one stool away nursing a whiskey. Ozzie looked his way and offered to buy him a drink. It was Ozzie's way of networking and tonight it would pay off.

Dave accepted his offer and Ozzie introduced himself, "Hi, my name's Ozzie Harper.

"My name's Dave Walker. Thanks for the drink.

"What brings you to Deer Lodge?" Dave asked Ozzie.

"I work for Highline Electric as a crane operator."

Dave couldn't believe his luck. "I may have a job to offer you. Shane McLane, the movie star, has a cabin here, and he needs a power line built to connect him to the local power company. I'm his general contractor and I need a couple of hands who know line work and can put in the power line for me." Dave waited for a response from Ozzie. Ozzie looked at Dave over his drink and said, "Maybe I can put a crew together. We'll have to talk about what the crew is going to make. They earn good money doing their day jobs. They won't drag their butts out on weekends to make minimum."

"I think you and I should come up with a fair price, then you pay your crew out of that figure. Whatever you think will be right."

"Okay," Ozzie said, "I can work with that. I'll need to see the ground we've got to cover, and I'll give you an estimate."

"When can you look at the site?" Dave inquired.

Bar noise around the two men was getting louder. More customers were coming in and it wouldn't be long before the band started warming up.

Ozzie offered to take a trip to Shane McLane's cabin with David the next day after work.

CHAPTER 4

Most of the people who attended the eulogy ended up at the Wilson home. Because of the generosity of her friends and neighbors Maggie had more than enough food and drink to do a respectable reception. Maggie knew some of the crowd had come for the food and drink and she accepted them the same as those who needed to be in her home to have a kind of release for their feelings over losing a friend they wouldn't be seeing again. Surrounded by the crowd Maggie felt less at a loss to have Filer and his family with her. Filer sat in the living room listening to what visitors had to say about Clayton.

About an hour into the reception Ozzie and Trina Harper arrived. Ozzie gave Maggie his condolences and left Trina in the kitchen with Abbey to deal with warming casseroles and washing empty serving dishes. In the living room, Ozzie again offered condolences-to Filer. With the formalities out of the way Ozzie accepted a whiskey from Filer. Then he did what he'd come to do, he offered Filer a job; or as close as he could come to offering him a job. He said Don Seifert, a General Superintendent for Highline Electric in Deer Lodge, Montana, needed a man.

"Don Seifert's a good boss and he needs a journeyman lineman to replace a hand that left Highline for another job." Ozzie reached into his shirt pocket and gave Filer one of Don Seifert's business cards; then they talked about a July 4th picnic they had spent with Clayton and Maggie. Ozzie and Clayton had become good friends because of Filer and had stayed in touch.

"Well 'Mad Dog', Trina and I have to get some sleep. We're heading back to Deer Lodge, tomorrow morning."

Filer had received the nickname 'Mad Dog' as an apprentice after threatening to go after a ground man working for him, "…like a junk yard dog," if he didn't straighten up. It turned out the man was a rapist, thief and part of a gang that killed a woman for her money and drugs.

"Thanks for coming Ozzie; it means a lot to me." Filer shook hands with Ozzie and was surprised when Ozzie hugged him briefly, and said, "I might have something else for you if you come to Montana."

Later, when guests had left the Wilson household, Filer sat with Maggie and listened to her plans for the future.

"I'll have Clayton's railroad survivor's pension and a life insurance policy. You don't need to worry on what I need. I have friends here in Riverview. I'll be fine."

With everyone else Filer maintained, but with Maggie he admitted he would miss Clayton.

"I'll miss him too, son. But we have to live our lives. You have to be strong to take care of Abbey and Kylie. As long as you take care of them the best you can, Clayton would approve."

"You know Mom we'd stay longer if we could, but we have to get back to Albany tomorrow."

"I know son," Maggie didn't speak for a minute and then said, "I want you to take anything of Clayton's you can use back to Albany with you." It was an offer she hoped would lessen Filer's grieving.

CHAPTER 5

Upon returning to Albany Filer found a letter in the mail from P. G. & E. explaining he would be on a seasonal layoff. It happened when the city spent its utility budget and had to lay workers off.

Some years earlier Filer had courted Abbey Lewis, a tall attractive blond divorcee, after he met her doing a Farewell Bend, Oregon job as an apprentice lineman. He proposed when he realized he needed Abbey in his life. Abbey said yes, and they got married in a civil ceremony in Elko, Nevada. Following their marriage he adopted Kylie, her nine year old daughter, and with a family to take care of he had hired on with a union job, working out of the 17th street headquarters of Portland Electric.

The new Wilson family sold Abbey's house in Ontario, Oregon and had bought their present home in Albany, Oregon.

As a journeyman lineman Filer did distribution work around Portland. Abbey got work as a checker with K & P Warehouse Groceries and Kylie attended school, made friends and grew into a confident eighteen-year old.

A seasonal layoff was nothing new to Filer, and normally Filer would have been content to wait until the union put him back to work, now he needed to be doing something. He told Abbey of Ozzie's offer of a job in Deer Lodge, Montana.

"You know I'm a boomer. Linemen take jobs where they can find them."

"You could wait until the union calls you back. We can get by."

"This doesn't have that much to do with getting by. I want to do something right now."

Abbey had seen this look on Filer before and she knew she wouldn't be able to talk him out of taking the job away from home. Her way of coping became one of accepting the inevitable.

"Kylie and I'll be alright. We survived in Ontario."

"You'll miss me," Filer teased Abbey.

"Only when something breaks down around here," Abbey teased.

"I wish you needed me more than just for doing chores," Filer said, then he smiled at Abbey and shrugged his shoulders, "I'd better call this Mr. Seifert and see if I can get the job he's offering."

Abbey nodded her reluctant approval.

Filer found the Highline Electric business card Ozzie had given him and dialed the number. A strong masculine voice came on the line.

"Don Seifert here."

"My name is Filer Wilson. Ozzie Harper gave me your business card and said you might have a job for me." Filer continued by explaining his situation. "I'm on a layoff now and I could use some work."

"Are you willing to come to Deer Lodge for as long as it takes to finish the job?"

"You bet."

"We work steel here. Have you worked steel?"

"Not on a regular basis. But I'll give you a good day's work-for a good day's pay."

"Okay then Mr. Wilson; come to Deer Lodge and we'll teach you how to work steel on a regular job."

After hanging up Filer wondered what it would mean to take this new job; the new bosses, going out of state, and some new drinking buddies. Abbey would love that. She kept him on a pretty tight allowance, but there was always money for a couple of beers.

Filer "Mad Dog" Wilson had all of these thoughts for a good reason. The job with Highline Electric would lead to a new phase of his working life. And if he thought he'd seen it all, he was in for a couple of surprises.

Abbey left the kitchen. She knew the call meant Filer would be away from home for the next year. Abbey thought she and Kylie had been alone before she married Filer, now she wondered why she felt so bad when she knew he'd be out of their lives again.

CHAPTER 6

After Abbey and Kylie helped Filer stock up his travel trailer, Filer was ready to go. Secretly he was anxious to travel. He was a boomer at heart. He had to be if he wanted to work as a lineman.

The Filer family spent a last night together. Early the next morning Filer hitched his pickup to the travel trailer and left Albany and his family behind.

Pulling the trailer, Filer made his way across Oregon farm fields and into the rolling hills of Montana, eventually arriving in Deer Lodge, Montana population 3,421, the home of Old Montana Prison. A couple of other museums attracted tourist dollars: Montana Auto Museum, The Frontier Montana Museum, and Yesterday's Playthings.

It was dark out so Filer pulled the trailer into a K.O.A. campground for one night until he could find a more permanent place.

After parking his trailer, Filer's old habits kicked in and he found a bar restaurant where he could get a meal. While he ate he heard a familiar sound. He listened for a minute and then really looked at the band and recognized Rip-It-Up Roberts, a guitarist and band leader he'd met working his first line job in Farewell Bend, Oregon.

CHAPTER 7

On stage Rip-It-Up announced the band would be taking a break. He had made it to the break without taking a drink. Now it would take all of his will power to keep from getting falling down drunk before the end of the evening.

Harold Roberts needed a woman in his life. If his former wife, Leslie hadn't abused their financial situation he would have happily overlooked her affairs. He didn't believe in a double standard. He knew Leslie was aware of his own excursions outside the bonds of marriage. Now that they were divorced he was depressed. As an aging musician it wasn't as easy to attract female company as it had once been.

Leslie Brower had long brunette hair and stunning blue eyes. When her girlfriends went to college she stayed in Ontario working at the local theater. She progressed from ticket taker at a single screen movie house to be the manager.

Being a manager gave her a level of status that she craved, but not the kind of money she wanted. Leslie went through a long list of men before she met Harold at the Wagon Wheel bar. She used all of her prowess to marry the musician just on the edge of losing his fifteen minutes of fame.

Nancy Sterling, night manager of the Broken Arrow, liked to watch Harold on stage; but she wouldn't admit she had a thing for the musician, even to herself. One thing she didn't like about Harold was his drinking, and on this evening she noticed Harold hadn't had anything to drink. Nancy also knew about Harold's recent divorce and attributed his drinking to the divorce.

CHAPTER 8

Listening to the country rock Roberts liked to play Filer looked around the bar and saw a table filled with construction types. When he finished eating Filer introduced himself to the table of construction workers. It turned out they were a footing crew for Highline Electric.

One of the men invited Filer to have a seat. Once he was seated Filer stopped a cocktail waitress and ordered another pitcher of beer for the table.

The man Filer assumed to be the big man at the table introduced himself. "My name's Briggs," he said and held his hand across the table filled with empty beer bottles and full ashtrays, to shake Filer's hand. "This is Harris," Briggs introduced the man sitting next to him, and followed by pointing around the table, "That's Solanski." A blond headed blued eyed man tipped his beer toward Filer. Briggs gestured to the next man, "And that's O'Conner."

Briggs announced to the table, "Hey, listen up. The next round is on 'Mad Dog' Wilson." Then he spoke to Filer. "I heard about you from the Oz man. He says you're a good hand. He also said you like to run ex-cons; something about a woman being killed by one of your ground men."

Filer sipped his beer, and then said, "I didn't hire the crew. I just kept them working" All eyes were now on the tall bearded man. Filer continued, "The ex-con wasn't the worst hand I've ever had and he sure wasn't the best. But Ozzie probably told you the whole story."

"The Oz man is a good ole boy. He's told us one or two tales."

Filer drank his beer and listened.

"Ozzie runs a crane for the erection crew. They follow us. We clean sites and get them squared away before the assembly and stacking crews get to them."

Briggs asked, "Do you know what crew you'll be on?"

"I don't know yet. The General Superintendent, Don Seifert told me he'd put me to work. My experience is mostly on wooden jobs. I've done distribution and transmission. I told Seifert: 'I'll give you a good day's work for a good day's pay.'"

Filer finished his beer and stood up to leave.

Briggs said, "The Oz man will be real mad at me if I don't tell him you're here. Where are you staying, 'Mad Dog'?"

"I'm at the K.O.A. campground temporarily. I'll be moving to another campground as soon as I find out what's close to work."

After the tall bearded man left the bar, Harris commented to Briggs, "So that's 'Mad Dog' Wilson. He seems like a good ole boy. At least he's good for a round or two of beers."

Filer found his way back to the K.O.A. campground and was soon relaxing in his recliner.

"S.O.S., the same old shit," Filer reflected as he settled into his recliner. "At least I won't have to relearn that part of line work," was Filer's last thought as he fell asleep.

CHAPTER 9

The next morning Filer was startled awake by a banging on his front door. The banging filled the trailer like the noise from a kid beating a garbage can with a stick.

"What the hell?" Filer said. He rolled out of bed and went to the door in his underwear. If missionaries were at the door they should know better than waking a man at this hour.

When Filer opened the door he was surprised to see Ozzie.

"Come on Filer, we're burning day light. Get dressed; I've got a surprise for you."

"How did you find me?" Filer got out as Ozzie followed him into the small but cozy interior of the Nomad trailer.

"Sean Briggs called me last night. He couldn't wait to give me the news you arrived in Deer Lodge. He told me you were in the K.O.A. temporarily. How many pickups have Oregon license plates in this campground? So here I am."

Filer showered and brushed his beard while Ozzie waited patiently.

"Okay old man, what's this big surprise of yours? And do we at least have time for a cup of coffee?"

"A cup of coffee will be alright, but we better hold off on breakfast."

Ozzie and Filer climbed into Ozzie's pickup. Ozzie pretended to be busy driving and let Filer watch the scenery.

After a ten minute drive Ozzie turned off the highway and took a side road to a forest service station. The station had an airstrip occupied by a small forest service aircraft.

"That's our ride 'Mad Dog'. I hope you're not too hung over to appreciate going up."

Filer sat speechless for a minute, and then followed Ozzie to the small plane on the runway.

"This is Lucille," Ozzie introduced Filer to the red headed pilot. "Her father taught her to fly. Now she works for the forest service."

"We're ready Lucille," Ozzie said after he and Filer were buckled in.

"Where are we going?" Filer wanted to know.

"I thought you might like to see how this job is laid out."

"This will be a first," Filer said.

Lucille gunned the small plane down the runway and lifted into the blue Montana sky.

Filer sat quietly watching the city of Deer Lodge grow smaller and give way to dry rolling hills and green pine forests.

From his window seat in the plane, Filer made a mental note of the project Ozzie was showing him.

As an eagle could fly the tower sites it would see a line of completed towers, towers assembled but not yet erected, and sites cleared with footings and bundles of steel waiting for assembly extending for thirty miles. The actual ribbon of rough graded company road connecting the tower sites weaved back and forth as if it had been dropped from above and floated down in a tangle touching each site.

From past experience Filer knew driving to each site might mean adding up to an hour a day of work time.

After Lucille had flown them on a round trip over the cleared tower sites below, Filer commented, "That's some playground Highline has down there."

"'Mad Dog', you haven't lost your way with words," Ozzie spoke over his shoulder.

After making a lower pass over the line of sites, the three sat in silence as Lucille banked the plane and started flying back towards the forest service airstrip.

"Here we are," Lucille informed Ozzie and Filer when she brought the plane to stop on the runway.

"Thanks for the tour darlin', Filer slipped unconsciously into the Filer charm mode.

"No need to darlin' me 'Mad Dog', my husband is the Head Forester; but it was nice meeting you."

Chapter 10

Harold Roberts' parents were both teachers. As an only child he received all of their attention; and when he showed a musical aptitude at an early age, they arranged for private piano lessons. Harold loved the lessons and didn't need to be forced to practice.

Harold senior was a high school history teacher. He was also a conservative republican who did his own investing. Instead of two week vacations, he took his family on long weekends to close by attractions. With the money saved he accumulated an impressive portfolio.

Jamine Roberts taught third grade in a city elementary. She loved her husband and son and made a good home for them. An intelligent woman, she reserved part of her salary for her own personal use. In reality, she spent most of this money on home improvements and her son.

With a different set of parents Harold Jr. could have been spoiled. Since both of his parents were successful teachers and had learned how to maintain well ordered classrooms, they applied their skills to raise Harold to be a well adjusted child.

In elementary school Harold was smaller than his classmates. He made up for his size by exploiting his extroverted personality. In class he clowned around, always getting teachers and fellow students laughing. On the playground, Harold tried to out think, or if that failed, to out run bullies. He generally succeeded with one tactic or the other.

Harold kept up his piano lessons and took up the guitar when he got interested in country western music. All through high school, encouraged by his parents, Harold participated in piano recitals. He succeeded well enough to win a music scholarship to Oregon State University in Corvallis, Oregon.

In his sophomore year, Harold's future as a classical musician took a turn for the worst. During a recital Harold stood up in front of a crowded auditorium, tore up his sheet music and did his impression of Jerry Lee Lewis.

Harold's advisor advised him he had lost his scholarship. His former classmates called him Rip-It-Up Roberts, and the nick name stayed with him. He never told his parents he had formed a garage band and was playing local gigs in and around Eugene.

CHAPTER 11

Abbey Wilson could have been a stay at home mom. That would have made Filer happy, but it wasn't what Abbey wanted. She had lived as a single parent making her own way and supporting Kylie long enough so that it was in her blood to be independent. When Filer got a job in Portland they discussed their future. Deciding to buy a house in Albany, not that far from Portland seemed like the logical next step.

With Kylie working at Sears, Abbey could work at K & P with a clear conscious. Her first job at K & P was as a checker. Abbey worked as a checker for six months until the manager noticed how good she was balancing her till. He offered to promote her to bookkeeper and she accepted. As a bookkeeper she made a little more pay and did her work in the customer service office. That's when her trouble started.

Stewart Parry, a single man, at age thirty-seven fancied himself to be a ladies man. Contrary to his perception, Stewart had the physique of a man going into middle age as a softy. And his idea of work place relations, where in, no woman could resist him was betrayed by his meager charms. Early on a Friday the produce manager came into the customer service office and leaned over Abbey's shoulder. He was too close to her, so she scooted as far away from him as she could in her chair.

Stewart moved with her and said, "What can I do for you Abbey? I'm in the store everyday."

"My God," Abbey said, "you can back off Stewart. You know I'm married; and I've got enough to do here without you hanging over me."

"Whoa, you've got me wrong Abbey. I just want to promote employee unity," Stewart took a step back from Abbey, but kept a smirky expression on his face.

"I finally get away from smart-ass customers and now I have to put up with Stewart," Abbey thought.

"I'll be here every day if you change your mind," Stewart crowed.

"Don't hold your breath. Wait, on second thought, do hold your breath," Abbey said.

Seth Hardwick, the store manager, came into the office. He saw a stupid look on produce manager Parry's face. "Don't you have something to do, Stewart?"

Stewart said, "No, I'm all caught up."

"Stewart, let me put it this way, go water some vegetables, or polish apples, or do whatever it is you do when you're pretending to be busy."

Stewart leered at Abbey with a lame expression and then at Seth before he left the office.

"Thanks Seth," Abbey said.

Seth replied, "Stewart is as fresh as his produce and he can be just as rotten as a crate of lettuce that's gone bad. He's the owner's nephew and I didn't have any choice when he was hired. If he comes in here and starts bothering you again give me a call on the intercom. Say you need customer service, and I'll come."

Abbey worked on the store accounts thinking, "Stewart had better hope Filer is never here when he pulls that kind of crap."

With the image of Filer in mind Abbey smiled and felt better.

CHAPTER 12

Ozzie drove Filer back to his trailer.

"Thanks for the tour Ozzie."

"How about dinner tonight, Trina would love to see you. Come over Filer, you're here alone. You could use a good home cooked meal."

"Sure Ozzie. I'll come.

"Good, I'll draw you a map. When you get settled, come over at about seven o'clock." Ozzie took a piece of paper out of his glove box and drew a simple map on it. He added his address and telephone number to the paper and handed it to Filer. "Call me if you get lost."

"Do you want me to bring anything?"

"Just bring an appetite.

Filer knew he was supposed to bring at least a six pack of beer.

"Okay Ozzie, I'll be there at about seven."

Ozzie got back in his dually and drove off. Filer went into his trailer and sat down. As he studied the piece of paper with the map on it Filer thought even if he was having dinner with Ozzie and Trina, he didn't like being away from Abbey and Kylie; but he had to make a living. Then he recalled that Ozzie hadn't mentioned the extra thing.

Whatever the next months brought, Filer's family would be first in his mind. But he knew Abbey could take care of Kylie and herself whether she wanted to or not. And he also remembered the first advice Ozzie had given him as an apprentice a long time ago: "Once you get on the job, line work requires all of your attention. If you start letting your attention wonder, you are an accident waiting to happen." Filer had learned that lesson well in the past years. Men who worked with him, and later, for him burned poles, suffered high voltage burns, and other work related accidents, some fatal.

Line work also took a toll on a lineman's body. When a young lineman started he treated his body like an indestructible machine that could accomplish work it wasn't meant to handle. If a young man was lucky, he learned early on to take care of his machine; if he didn't he suffered the consequences. This simple fact was why Filer was sitting in his easy chair feeling tired before his first day on the job. A man had to learn to pace himself. He not only had to learn to pace himself, he had to teach those around him to pace their selves as well. Most crew supervisors knew this too, even if they didn't admit it. It was called working smart.

"I've got a lot to do today," Filer decided, "I should get started."

CHAPTER 13

Don Seifert reminded Filer of his grandfather who had been a water warden, or ditch rider in rural Idaho. Grandfather Wilson was a no-nonsense man who had to deal with hard nosed farmers who tried to cheat each other to get more than their share of irrigation water.

Unlike his grandfather, Don Seifert had a friendly smile when he looked at the application Filer Wilson had filled out.

"Are you a union man?" he asked.

"I've worked union jobs."

"We're non-union, but we pay you a journeyman lineman's wage. If you do a good day's work we won't have any problems."

Seifert looked at Filer. Filer replied, "I came here to work. I've got a family back in Albany. If I'd waited for the union to get me another job it could have been a day, a week, a month or six months before I went back to work. We need the money now."

"Good, that's what I wanted to hear." Seifert went on to explain how he would break Filer into Highline Electric. "What I want to do is start you on assembly. When you've done assembly on a couple of structures we'll put you on stacking. And after that, when we get an opening we'll put you on a wire crew."

Seifert looked at Filer as if he was looking for a quality of leadership that could be read in appearances alone and then said, "If you work out on a wire crew we'll try you as a foreman with more pay. This job may last another year. When the job is done we'll keep you on for the next job."

"I'm ready to go to work," Filer promised. He knew the less he said in this first interview the better off he'd be. A boss wanted to hear a hand understood what he'd just said and that the hand agreed to what he'd explained. At this point all a hand could do was to get to work without having a boss lose patience. What he'd said was a pretty standard hiring speech. Filer had heard the same speech before on almost every job he'd worked. Now the ball was in Seifert's court.

"Okay Mr. Wilson, do you have any questions?"

Filer did need some basic information. "My trailer is in a K.O.A. campground right now. Is there a trailer court nearer to the job than the K.O.A.?"

"There's a nice trailer court within walking distance of the show-up site in Garrison. Why don't you get settled in there and I'll met you at the show-up site tomorrow morning."

Filer had been hired on a trial basis.

CHAPTER 14

At first glance Filer decided Seifert was right-the trailer court he'd recommended was a well established area with tall cottonwood trees providing shade and a stream running between the access road and the court.

The nearby town of Garrison consisted of a small general store and five or six residential homes.

After working out a rental agreement with the trailer court manager Filer pulled into his space. Filer noticed an angler trying his luck close to where his trailer was now installed. Even though he wasn't a fisherman Filer wished the angler luck.

It took the rest of the morning and most of the afternoon for Filer to get settled into the trailer court by the show-up site. He made the electrical and sewer hook-ups. Filer speculated as he completed these tasks that it was true about trailers-if you weren't working underneath them, you were working on top of them. In other words they took a lot of maintenance. The good things about living in a trailer were privacy, convenience of being close to the job, and it could be more of a home than a motel room.

Once he had the trailer hooked up, Filer used a pay phone in the trailer park office to call Abbey long distance collect.

CHAPTER 15

Abbey accepted the charges and listened to Filer explain his living arrangements.

"Hey darlin', I'm hired and all set up and ready to go to work. Ozzie's working here and I'm going to dinner at his place tonight. He's here with Trina," Filer said the last with a little homesickness in his voice.

Abbey replied, "Filer honey, I'm glad you're okay. Let me know if you need anything. Do you have enough money? If you need more, you can spend a little more. Take your allowance early."

"Thanks, but I'm okay so far. I'll let you know if I need anything. How's Kylie?"

"Kylie is fine. She misses you. She won't say it, but I know she does."

Filer realized he had made a mistake as soon as he said, "I saw Rip-It-Up Roberts playing at a local bar and restaurant last night."

Abbey didn't say anything.

"Are you there darlin'?"

"Filer don't darlin' me. You know what I think of Rip-It-Up. Stay away from that man. I know you won't, but I wish you would."

"Damn," Filer thought, "I could have talked all day without telling her about Rip-It-Up."

"Don't worry Abbey; I'll be too tired to get in trouble with Rip-It-Up."

"Since when did being tired keep you out of the bars at night?"

"True," Filer admitted to himself. Then he said, "You don't give me enough money to get in that much trouble hon." Abbey didn't miss Filer's humorous tone.

Abbey came back, "If I didn't give you any money you could still find a way to get in trouble; like borrowing money from Harold Rip-It-Up Roberts, your old loan sharking friend."

"You know I paid that off and I'm a reformed man now."

"They don't call you 'Mad Dog' because you sit at home meditating at night. Now I mean it-stay away from Rip-It-Up."

Filer soothed Abbey by telling her he loved her and Kylie and wished he could be with them in Albany; and that he wouldn't get in any trouble.

By the time their conversation was over he'd spent five dollars in long distance charges.

Filer took a break in his trailer and wondered again what the extra thing Ozzie mentioned might be.

CHAPTER 16

Night life in Deer Lodge had two faces. Happily married locals settled in front of their T.V. sets and watched their favorite shows. After prime time ended, a good night's sleep with conjugal activity as a bonus completed the evening.

For the other face, single construction workers gathered in local restaurants and then went to bars. The entertainment wasn't up to prime time T.V. standards, but the chances of the audience becoming a part of the entertainment were much greater. Drunks yelled at other drunks, and anyone else catching their attention.

Waitresses and barmaids took their chances serving the drunks, and some ended up getting closer than they expected to their customers. The next morning could be awkward.

Rip-It-Up and his Misfits provided background noise for the shouting drunks and general clamor of the Broken Arrow's regular crowd. A few couples occupied the dance floor seeming to feel the music over the yelling and screaming.

CHAPTER 17

Filer followed Ozzie's directions to an R.V. park on the edge of Deer Lodge. He parked his truck in front of the R.V. beside Ozzie's pickup and an older Ford pickup. He carried a six pack of beer to the R.V.'s front steps and knocked on the door.

Trina Harper opened the door and spread her arms wide for Filer. As she gave him a big hug she said, "Filer Wilson, how are you doing?" She didn't say it, but Filer knew she was referring to Clayton's passing. Without any pause she continued, "How are Abbey and Kylie? It's really nice to see you."

By the time Trina had wound down, she'd taken Filer's beer into the kitchen, handed him a refrigerated bottle and led him into the living room where Ozzie and a man Filer didn't know were already seated.

Trina asked Filer, "How did you like your tour this morning?"

"It was fun, wasn't it 'Mad Dog'?" Ozzie answered before Filer could say anything.

"It was the best flight I've had since I got here in Deer Lodge."

"I knew you'd like it Buddy."

"Why do you stay with him Trina? There's got to be a better man out there somewhere?" Filer said with a straight face.

"He pays the bills and he's fun to be around once in a while," Trina answered.

"She knows me Filer. I'm the man."

"You're the man," Filer agreed.

Ozzie introduced Filer to the smiling stranger. "Filer this is Shane McLane," Ozzie stopped as if the name was supposed to mean something to him.

When Filer couldn't place the stranger, the man stopped smiling and looked at Ozzie.

"Come on Filer. This is Shane McLane, you know, the action adventure star; *Kill or be Killed, Death of a Dealer.*"

"Oh that Shane McLane," Filer stumbled.

Shane McLane still wasn't smiling.

"Here's the deal Filer," Ozzie explained, "Shane is building a cabin outside Deer Lodge. The local power company has a waiting list for private power lines. Shane doesn't want to wait that long so he wants to hire us to do his power line."

Shane put on a smile and nodded his head.

"Well Ozzie," Filer said, "I want this job with Highline Electric. Let me work for a week or so before I think about doing the power line."

Ozzie added more information, "The cabin won't be ready for electricity for a month and we still have to find another lineman. Oh, and Filer," Ozzie said looking in Shane's direction, "Shane wants to go up a pole or two to see what line work is like."

Filer looked at Shane.

The movie star explained, "I play an action hero in the movies. I do whatever stunts the director and producers will let me do." He lifted his bottle of beer and shuffled the coaster back and forth. "Of course they don't let me do the dangerous stuff," Shane admitted.

Filer sat with a stunned look on his face.

"So Filer," Ozzie told me you're nick name is 'Mad Dog'. He said to ask you about Farewell Bend."

Filer continued sitting in silence, then he said, "You know I think I did see one of your pictures. My wife liked it. Me, I'm not a big movie fan so I'll take her word for it that you're okay."

Trina called them to the dinner table. Trina had cooked a roast with potatoes and gravy. As they passed the pot roast, mashed potatoes, brown gravy, and green beans, around they told stories of their past experiences with different electrical construction companies.

Shane impressed Filer by being a good listener.

After dinner Shane got up and shook Ozzie's hand and then Filer's. "That was a great dinner Trina. We'll have to do it again when I get the cabin up and running." Shane turned to Filer and said, "I'm looking forward to going up some poles with you.

You don't need to show me out Ozzie," Shane said and left the three friends sitting at the dinner table.

"What do you think Filer? We can make some money on this one."

"How do we make money on this one?"

"Hell man, Shane's a millionaire who doesn't know what to do with all the money he's making. He'll pay top dollar to finish this job for him."

Filer smiled, "Who's buying the beer?"

Ozzie returned the smile and said, "Of course Shane McLane is buying the beer."

Filer took another sip of beer and stared at Ozzie over his beer bottle, "As long as the big movie star does what he's told and stays out of the way."

"Sure, sure 'Mad Dog', I'll be sure to keep Shane on a short leash. One more thing 'Mad Dog': Shane and Rip-It-Up Roberts are friends from when Rip-It-Up was doing gigs in L.A. and he wants Harold to be our ground man."

"I don't know Ozzie," Filer frowned thinking of what he'd promised Abbey, "did you scout out people to make the job harder?"

Back at his trailer Filer called Abbey and told her about Ozzie's job offer working for Shane McLane. He didn't mention Rip-It-Up would be on the crew.

Abbey didn't say anything about Shane; she only said, "Honey, I know you're worried about paying the bills. You shouldn't worry so much. I've got everything under control."

As Filer listened to Abbey he could hear relief just underneath her reassurances about having their situation under control.

CHAPTER 18

Rip-It-Up Roberts made it to the Broken Arrow at the last minute to do a fast warm-up with the Misfits. He decided that he'd try playing without alcohol, again. He refused a wine cooler sent over by the bartender. When the warm-up instrumental was done, applause drifted to the stage in small whiffs.

"Okay," Rip-It-Up said, "let's do *Harden My Heart*." He started the band into the evening ahead playing with gusto. The members of the band smiled at one another and wondered if the mood would last.

A cheer went up from the crowd and several drinks for the band arrived on stage. Harold ignored the temptation for the first set, then he got thirsty when the band came back on stage and said, "What the hell, I'm a musician not a saint." He picked up a Bloody Mary and took a fast drink, then finished the rest in another swallow. "That'll be it," Harold promised himself.

With the Misfits warmed up and ready for the long evening ahead, Harold slowed down and introduced his band mates. He gestured to the drummer and said, "The best drummer this side of Bozeman-Johnny Taylor." Rip-It-Up waited while the crowd clapped and yelled for Taylor, and he did a slow roll on the drums.

When the bar noise settled Rip-It-Up pointed to the bass guitarist and said, "This is Jackson Vaughn, give him a big hand."

Jackson played a chord on his guitar while the crowd cheered for him.

Rip-It-Up and the men he'd just introduced had been together since he formed the band and dropped out of college. He considered them to be family.

CHAPTER 19

Filer met Don Seifert at the show-up site the morning after dinner with Ozzie and Trina. He parked his truck beside Seifert's company truck and rolled down his window. Seifert lowered his window and said, "Good morning Mr. Wilson let's get you to a tower site."

Seifert drove a forest road through foothills and then climbed higher up a mountain until they arrived at a site where an assembly crew worked.

Working steel is more complicated and more dangerous, in different ways than working wood. The given is electricity-once steel or wood structures are up and the lines are hot.

With steel, fingers and hands are always at risk to be pinched, smashed or amputated. All of these accidents can happen hours, not minutes from the most rudimentary medical help. Of course the more regular body functions are done in the immediate area surrounding the work site. No porta-potties are paid for by the electrical construction outfits.

These facts are what Filer knew and expected from his years of experience as a working lineman.

When Filer got out of Don Seifert's pickup and saw the piles of steel setting beside the footings already in place, he didn't know to ask whether the steel beams were made in the United States or Japan. Later he learned steel parts fabricated in the States left a lot to be desired when compared with the precision construction of Japanese steel parts.

Mr. Seifert told Filer, "I'm going to turn you over to the foreman Todd. He'll get you settled in. Todd has worked for Highline Electric

Construction for six years. He knows steel construction. Learn what you can from him until I can find a place for you working wire."

Seifert motioned for Todd to come over to his truck and introduced him to Filer, "Filer will be working on your crew for the next month or so. His nickname is 'Mad Dog', and he's a journeyman lineman. You might learn a little from him if you keep your eyes open.

Okay then men, that's all I've got for you."

Seifert turned his pickup around and gunned back down the dirt trail towards the comforts of his office in Deer Lodge.

Chapter 20

Todd and Filer sized one another up without saying anything. Filer noticed a gold ring on Todd's left hand, then Todd moved, turning his back on Filer, expecting the experienced journeyman lineman to follow him and returned to the loose bundles of steel.

"Filer, you'll be building dog legs with Chester." This served as Filer's introduction to a man standing by a bundle of steel. "This work is hard, but it doesn't have to be difficult," Todd said, leaving the two men together.

Chester looked to be in his late thirties. He had a strong upper body and a slim waist with the beginnings of a beer belly. Chester greeted Filer by saying, "If you're a journeyman lineman you've learned one or two things working with wire. Working assembly is probably a lot closer to the ground than you're used to." Chester went on explaining, "What we do first is shake the steel out." Filer gave him a questioning look.

"What that means is that we get the steel for the dog leg and separate it from steel for the rest of the tower." Chester checked Filer with a quick glance and Filer nodded. Chester continued, "When we get it sorted out we'll start bolting it together-loosely. Once we've completed the dog leg we'll help put arms and the cage together.

We work until twelve o'clock and break for a half hour lunch. If you have to go, we've got the whole wide woods to do it in. But be careful you don't step in someone else's toilet break. We don't take time for anything fancy like a slit trench."

While Filer and Chester worked the dog leg, Todd and Parker, the other crew member, worked a cage. A third team worked the arms.

At twelve o'clock the different teams working the bundles of steel stopped working and took their lunch breaks.

Filer waited for it. As the new man, the rest of the crew would want to know who he was. This kind of knowledge didn't come from a resume. First they would want to know how he came to be called 'Mad Dog'.

Todd started in a voice intended to put Filer on the spot, "Seifert called you 'Mad Dog'; is that supposed to mean something 'Mad Dog'?"

"I don't suppose I could just eat my lunch in peace?" Filer said.

"Sure you can eat your lunch in peace. Just tell us why we should all be calling you 'Mad Dog', 'Mad Dog'."

Filer decided to see if he could get away with the short version. "On my first job as an apprentice the boss put me charge of an auger. Two of the hands on my crew started in on one another, and I told them I'd come after them like a junk yard dog if they didn't back off."

"Well, 'Mad Dog'," Todd said, "I just wanted to hear it from the Dog's mouth. We know all about you, Filer "Mad Dog" Wilson. Ozzie, the Oz man bragged a whole lot about working that job with you. When we get to drinking we get to hear it all over again about the convict, the crooked junk dealer, the gang of copper thieves, and how you saved a pregnant woman from being electrocuted and got electrocuted yourself. Welcome to Highline Electrical Construction 'Mad Dog'."

The men finished eating lunch in the mountain stillness, interrupted only by chipmunks chattering back and forth.

Filer thought the clear, dry mountain air smelling of pine trees compared favorably with the wetter weather in Albany. He finished his sandwich and coffee from a thermos, and had a few minutes to think of Abbey and Kylie. Once that thought passed he wondered about what was expected of him after today's work on the mountain was finished. For the last year he'd had an excuse not to go drinking because he was needed at home by his wife and daughter. Although he hadn't always used that excuse, especially when he wanted to go drinking.

During the afternoon, Chester and Filer completed a dog leg and then helped other teams work on arms and the cage.

After they finished for the day Todd asked Filer what he thought of assembly.

"It's the most fun a man can have with his clothes on," Filer smiled in reply.

Todd invited Filer to sit in the front of the crew cab for the ride off of the mountain. "How about taking a trip to Fred's in Missoula for a little T and A.?" Todd invited Filer. "It's a rare treat," he encouraged Filer.

The tower site, only recently ringing with the sound of wrenches tightening bolts, fell silent. No night watchman guarded the site. Its isolation provided it protection and guaranteed its safety. What the assembly crew left behind would be there for the stacking crew in the morning.

Back in Deer Lodge day shifts changed places with swing shifts. Soon enough the grocery stores, restaurants and bars would be hosts to the day shift workers. For the day shift it would be a quick trip home to clean up, and then they would be out their doors to enjoy the fruits of their labors.

CHAPTER 21

In Albany, Abbey Wilson completed some last additions in her books and tidied up her work space before leaving the store. Stewart, the produce man, observed Abbey through the small customer service window. He hadn't gotten to be a manager by giving up on his ideas; some who knew Stewart might call his ideas obsessions.

His most recent obsession of stepping in for the absent Filer Wilson in regards to Abbey's love life overwhelmed him at times. She always refused his suggestions in a manner that didn't leave any room for misunderstanding, but no was where negotiations started wasn't it.

Abbey stepped out of the customer service office and headed for the supermarket's front door. Out of nowhere, Stewart appeared blocking the door.

"Hey Abbey," Stewart started his spiel, "how about having dinner with me tonight? My treat," Stewart offered, as if the price of a free dinner, paid for by him would seal the deal.

"Stewart," Abbey began in as serious a manner as she could summon, "I'm tired. I have to get home and fix dinner for Kylie. I'm married and I want you to get out of my way. Is there any part of what I just said that wasn't clear?" Abbey gave Stewart a drop dead stare as she pushed past him and went out the automatic open store doors. Stewart remained inside the supermarket as if waiting for Abbey to come back and say she'd only been joking.

On her drive home, Abbey thought Stewart had to be a lost cause. "Hasn't he ever heard, 'There are a lot of fish in the sea'," Abbey laughed, "Probably wouldn't relate to that because he's a produce man."

Abbey's thoughts turned to Filer. If Filer occasionally went out for a beer after work, it was because he didn't have family waiting for an evening meal at his trailer.

Abbey had made friends with the female cashiers at the store and took her afternoon breaks with one or the other of the women if their lunch breaks were scheduled at the same time. This wasn't the same as having a beer or two after work, but she recalled when she and Gale Jordan, an old friend in Ontario, had gone out drinking and dancing after work. They had been out together when she first met Filer. She still kept in touch with Gale. Gale had a new boy friend. Of course Gale always had a new boyfriend. Whether that was Gale's fault or not Abbey had given up trying to figure out.

Now when Abbey got the urge for a night out it certainly wasn't with Stewart. It wouldn't have been him when she was single. She could see herself in a quiet bar drinking a glass of wine with a female friend who knew what it was like to be separated by necessity from a husband. They could discuss kids, bills, and romance, probably in that order.

On this particular evening Abbey was definitely looking forward to getting Kylie's dinner and then some serious relaxing in front of the T.V. set.

CHAPTER 22

Todd dropped the crew off at the show up area. As Filer got out of the company truck Todd said, "Get cleaned up and I'll come by and pick you up for the trip to Fred's."

Filer was curious about Fred's so he agreed to the trip. Like most of the linemen he got bored sitting in his trailer. A man could only watch so much T.V., or read so many Louie L'Amour novels. Before he showered Filer picked up a special family photo in which he had posed with Abbey and Kylie.

Thirty minutes later Todd knocked on Filer's door and came into the trailer while Filer put on his boots.

The two men spent the time it took driving to Missoula talking about leaving their families to come and work in Montana.

Todd had a wife and teenage son in Utah. He assured Filer he wasn't a Mormon. The way he talked Filer got the sense that he missed his family.

Filer reciprocated by telling Todd about Abbey and Kylie.

Inside the city limits of Missoula Todd easily found his way to Fred's. A neon light outside the bar proclaimed LIVE NUDE STRIPPERS.

"Abbey definitely wouldn't approve of this," Filer thought.

Todd found a space in a parking lot filled with working hands' rigs.

"Come on 'Mad Dog'. There are live strippers inside," Todd quoted off of the neon sign.

A huge black man stood guard at the door to Fred's, collecting a five dollar fee just to get into the establishment.

"That's a little pricey," Filer complained to Todd.

"Quit your bitching," Todd said and pushed through the double doors into the darkened interior of the strip joint.

As Filer's eyes adjusted to the dim bar lights, his attention was drawn to a runway sprouting duel chrome poles. Two young women were wrapped around the poles in various stages of undress.

The chairs and tables closest to the runway were occupied by men waving dollar bills to get the strippers' attention. Filer turned to Todd and saw a certain look in his eyes that told Filer it was going to be an exciting night for him.

Todd found an empty table two rows back from the runway. He still didn't look like he had given up on getting a front row seat. "We'll have to wait until one of the tables next to the runway opens up," Todd advised Filer.

Filer could tell Todd had been to Fred's before and hadn't had his fill of tits and ass yet. And that seemed a little strange to Filer if Todd was a happily married man. Maybe the word strange had something to do with it-as in strange stuff.

Soon enough a topless cocktail waitress named Shirley came to their table to take their drink orders. Shirley had brunette hair and honey brown eyes. With her fine figure, she would have been hard to miss with all of her clothes on. Filer ordered a beer, planning to stay sober in case he had to drive back to Deer Lodge.

Todd ordered a Seven and Seven, and tried to pat Shirley on the butt, but she was too fast for him and got away un-patted.

The runway strippers were getting near the end of their number and as a finale they took off their pull away G-strings revealing strategically placed pasties. The women then ran off the runway with tips from their G-strings filling both hands. The crowd whistled and hollered for more.

Shirley came back to Filer's and Todd's table with their drinks.

"That's a pretty good act your strippers have," the always friendly Filer commented to Shirley.

"You think that's good. Do you want to see a dragon's tail?" Shirley asked Filer, and pointed to the head of a full color, fire breathing dragon tattooed on her flat stomach.

"Yes I would Shirley," Filer said.

Todd had his eyes on a table about to be emptied by the runway and wasn't paying any attention to the exchange between Filer and Shirley.

Shirley moved closer to Filer until she was standing between his knees, and then pulled her spandex shorts outward and down enough so Filer could see where the dragon's tail disappeared into her bikini shaved pubis.

Filer stared at the dragon until Shirley snapped her spandex shorts closed and leaned forward and whispered, "If you want to see more, I'll be off work at two a.m."

"I'll have to think about it Shirley," Filer said not holding out much promise to Shirley. Along with the price of the drinks Filer slipped Shirley a twenty dollar bill.

"What was that all about?" Todd wanted to know.

"Shirley and I were just getting to know each other a little better," Filer answered with a smile.

A disheveled man wearing a gray cotton hooded sweater and aviator sunglasses left a runway table. Todd grabbed his Seven and Seven and almost knocked over the table they were sitting at getting to the empty table.

"This ought to be good," Filer said to himself, and wondered how long it would take Todd to decide whatever he was looking at-he'd seen it before.

Filer picked up his beer and moved to the empty table with Todd.

When the two men had settled into their seats another pair of dancers emerged on the runway from behind curtains blocking the view into the dressing room hallway.

The M.C. announced the pair as Phyllis and Daphne.

Daphne was a blond with small but perfect breasts, and a full body on a small, well muscled frame. Phyllis, a redhead with full breasts and long legs, moved down the runway and started dancing in front of Todd and Filer. Todd waved a single at the edge of the runway and Phyllis stooped down low so he could tuck it into her G-string. Then she was off to the other side of the runway dancing for a business type wearing a suit coat with a loosened tie.

"Damn," Todd said, "just when I was making headway."

"You wish," Filer thought, "I can't believe this guy is married, and now he's this desperate for a peak at naked."

Todd spoke in Filer's direction without taking his eyes off the runway, "So what do you think, 'Mad Dog'? Is Fred's worth the trip?"

Filer didn't say anything.

One of the strippers must have sensed Todd's eyes on her because she turned her back on the business man and came across the runway to dance in front of Todd and Filer. Her move put a huge smile on Todd's face.

Filer took a five dollar bill out of his pocket and held it up so Phyllis could see it. The attractive redhead moved to the edge of the runway and pulled her G-sting away from her thigh so Filer could place the five under the G-string. Phyllis smiled at Filer; and Todd, who was ready with another single.

Filer knew Abbey wouldn't approve of the way he was spending his allowance, but what the hell, he had to do something to keep his spirits up.

Shirley had been watching while Filer put the fiver in Phyllis' G-string and came back to his table.

"Hey Mr. Tall and Bearded Stranger," Shirley addressed Filer.

Todd spoke up, "This is 'Mad Dog' ma'am. And my name is Todd. I build steel towers and Mad Dog is a lineman."

Shirley barely glanced in Todd's direction and then said, "Well, 'Mad Dog', my stage name is Glitter and I can do better for you than Phyllis up there," after saying this Shirley, who's stage name was Glitter, leaned forward and put her breasts on either side of Filer's face. With Filer's beard brushing her cheeks Glitter whispered, "You earned this with the twenty and besides I wanted to see how your beard feels on my skin."

Filer knew either he would be let down this night, or Glitter would. With thoughts of Abbey in mind he decided he and Glitter were destined to be just friends. So that's the way he would play it.

Shirley had straightened up and backed away a step, waiting for Filer to say something.

"Glitter darlin', I don't get up here very often, but when I do, you and I are definitely going to be good friends. I need all the friends I can get in this world," Filer explained.

A look of disappointment passed over Glitter's face when she registered what Filer had just told her.

Todd acted like he'd had enough of Fred's and suggested they should start back to Deer Lodge. Filer agreed.

CHAPTER 23

Harold Roberts made it big for his allotted fifteen minutes of fame.

In 1975 he left Ontario, Oregon, on the advice of his manager, for L.A. He played in some warehouse dance clubs. And at the height of his popularity he made an album that sold well enough to be played at radio stations across the Pacific Northwest and California. His combination of country, rock and blues lasted a couple of months during which he met several aspiring actors including Shane McLane. Shane had just finished *Kill or be Killed*. A movie the critics and the public loved.

Rip-It-Up made the most of his popularity by spending his money on a stream of one night stands, a new Cadillac, and lots of drugs. Then, it seemed, at the height of his popularity it all came to an end and Rip-It-Up and the Misfits was replaced by the next hot band.

Harold's parents followed their son's brief career with foreboding. If they could have talked to him, they would have told him to put his money in mutual funds, or CD's. They were headed for their retirement years on social security, pensions, and cost of living raises, and they knew the importance of saving for the future.

Unfortunately for Harold, he made an effort to avoid his parents. They cramped his style. Now in his thirties, the money and the groupies were all behind him as well as a failed marriage. He'd only managed to hold onto the Cadillac, an iconic reminder of better days.

CHAPTER 24

At the end of a hard day's work following the excursion to Fred's, Filer showered and walked to the trailer park manager's office.

"Mr. Wilson, what can I do for you?"

"Hi darlin'," Filer began.

"Save the darlin' cowboy. My name's Hettie; and I'm here for business."

"You got it Hettie," Filer switched gears, "I need to get the telephone in my trailer turned on. Problem is, I leave early in the mornings and don't get back until after five o'clock. Could you do me a favor and call the telephone company for me. I'll leave a key with you so they can get into my trailer."

"I've done that for other tenants and they didn't even start out by calling me darlin' cowboy," Hettie smiled at Filer. She looked at his left hand and noticed his wedding ring. "I guess you're getting that phone so you can call your wife; how about letting me know if that gets to be too much of a chore cowboy."

It was Filer's turn to smile. "Not gonna happen Hettie. And my name is Filer or 'Mad Dog'," he said and handed Hettie a spare key. Hettie accepted the key and made a note to get Filer's phone turned on.

Filer called Abbey on the pay phone. He hoped it would be the last time he had to use it.

Abbey's phone rang twice and she picked it up, "Hi darlin', it's me. How are you doing?"

"I'm fine. I just got off work. I'm waiting for Kylie to get home before I start dinner. How are things in Montana?"

Filer explained, "I'm on an assembly crew building dog legs"

"Dog legs?"

"Dog legs are part of a steel tower. I'll show you one when I get back to Albany."

Filer switched into the concerned husband and father mode. "How are you two doing?"

"We're doing fine Filer. The bills are paid and we may even be able to put some money in the bank if you stay on with Highline."

Filer's conscious kicked at him when he remembered the money he'd given Glitter and the stripper. Then he said, "Well, you know I'll be here until they let me go."

"I know Filer. I love you."

"I love you too," Filer said, "I better get off now before I run up a big long distance bill again."

Filer listened to Abbey hang up and hoped she'd be okay until he could get back to Albany.

"I'd better have something to eat," Filer cautioned himself. He'd learned a thing or two concerning alcohol during his career as a hard charging lineman. Drinking on an empty stomach made for a worse than usual hangover the next morning. As he had been told, a full stomach absorbed some of the alcohol and limited the effects of a late night bender. He didn't plan on having more than a couple of beers with the crew after the previous late night at Fred's, but he'd told himself the same story on other occasions.

CHAPTER 25

Filer decided to have dinner at the Fireplace Inn. The Fireplace Inn cooked steaks and sea food. When Filer walked in he saw a water tank filled with live lobsters crawling across rocks on the bottom of the tank. A female hostess greeted him and showed him into a homey dining room. Three families sat at near by tables enjoying dinner. As Filer walked by the families he received stares from parents and kids. Apparently they'd never seen a man with a beard before. The hostess took Filer to a small table by a window.

"Your waitress will be here with a menu," the young woman said.

"Thanks," Filer replied. He watched traffic going by the restaurant while he waited.

His waitress came and recommended a special. Filer already had his mind made up.

"I'll take the New York cut steak, a baked potato and a cup of coffee."

"Okay sir, we'll have that right out for you."

Again Filer watched traffic. He thought of Ozzie having left over pot roast with Trina and wished he could be back in Albany having leftovers with Abbey and Kylie.

Ten minutes went by while Filer watched traffic and had more thoughts of being at home.

The waitress arrived with Filer's meal and a smile. When she arranged the plates on the table Filer woke up from his thoughts of home and said, "your tip is looking good darlin'."

The waitress soon returned with a pot of coffee and offered Filer a refill. Two refills later Filer had almost finished his dinner when he looked up from his meal and saw Shirley, a.k.a. Glitter, standing by this table.

It took Filer a moment to recognize the cleaned up young woman standing in front of him.

"Hi 'Mad Dog', how are you doing?" Shirley started what she hoped would be a friendly conversation.

"I'm fine. Sit down," Filer invited the cocktail waitress/stripper to his table.

"Thanks, I don't usually go out to dinner alone. Tonight I was hungry and didn't want to cook."

"I know what you mean," Filer agreed, "Sometimes you have to go out to get a good meal." What he said sounded lame to him, but he was married after all; and he didn't have to thrill every female with fancy talk.

"What did you have?"

"Just steak and a baked potato."

"That sounds good," Shirley said and stopped a passing waitress to take her order.

When Shirley had a cup of coffee she talked while Filer finished the last of his meal.

"Whenever I want to be just Shirley I come to Deer Lodge for a night off. You'd be surprised how often I get recognized in Missoula. I'm not famous but men who've seen me in Fred's do look at me twice when I'm out in public. And, I've seen men with their wives who definitely don't want me saying hi. That doesn't happen that often here in Deer Lodge."

Filer decided to be a good listener.

"You know, when I showed you my dragon I was a little drunk," Shirley confided. "Don't tell the manager at Fred's. We're not supposed to be drinking on the job."

"Don't worry," Filer said smiling, "your secret is safe with 'Mad Dog'."

Shirley still had more to say, "Even bad girls are looking for Mr. Right. Deep down they might not think they're good enough for Mr. Right, but that doesn't keep them from looking. The funny thing is:

good girls pick bad men because bad men don't have any reservations about hitting on good girls. Mr. Right is too busy being Mr. Right to go after the women who want him."

"You've thought about this a lot, haven't you?" Filer said.

"All of that thinking makes me believe you're the type of man bad girls aren't afraid of, and good girls think they can reform."

"So I'm Mr. Right?"

"Not exactly, you're just the kind of man most women can relate to."

"Very interesting," Filer said.

Glitter asked Filer about his job, "What do linemen do?"

Filer looked at Glitter and didn't want to give her a short answer. He wanted to impress her. "What do you think linemen do?"

"Something to do with power poles and electricity I guess," Glitter answered.

Filer smiled, "The Highline job is a steel job. On this job Highline has about forty people working thirty different tower sites. The hands are divided into footing crews, assembly crews, stacking crews and wire crews. I'm working assembly. I took the job because the General Superintendent told me he'd put me on a wire crew as soon as there is an opening." Filer stopped and looked at Glitter. "Are you bored, yet?"

If Glitter was bored she didn't admit it. She fluttered her eyelashes and shook her head from side to side.

"Okay then, there are a couple of different structures necessary to build a steel power tower. A footing pad is the base for the tower. Legs, dog legs, bodies, cages, arms and a goat's peak are all stacked together to make in-line towers, angle towers and anchor or terminal towers. Once the towers are assembled, stacked, and three phase, aluminum wire is added the job is done. There are a lot of other steps, but basically that's what goes into building a steel tower and adding power lines."

Glitter fluttered her eyelashes again and said, "The short version will do-for now."

The waitress came back with Shirley's dinner and poured Filer a final cup of coffee.

"You don't have to stay."

"Well, I'm meeting the crew at the Broken Arrow."

"Be careful there, the Arrow can get a little rowdy," Shirley warned.

"I hear you," Filer stood up and walked to the cash register where he paid both of their bills.

When Shirley finished her meal the waitress told her the man she'd been sitting with had paid for her meal.

Chapter 26

Filer parked across the street from the Arrow. He entered the dimly lit bar and scanned the packed tables looking for the Highline crew. It took him a minute or two for his eyes to adjust to the dim lights and smoke filled room, and then he saw Todd motioning him over with a raised arm.

Todd, Chester and Parker sat at a table near the stage. They'd been drinking since the band started playing an hour earlier. Cocktail waitresses circulated through the tables, filled mostly with construction workers, taking orders from the patrons shouting to be heard above the band.

"Hey 'Mad Dog'," Todd called out and the crew pulled out a chair for Filer.

Filer sat down and waved at a passing cocktail waitress, "Hi darlin', bring us another round, and I'd like a Budweiser in a bottle."

The cocktail waitress named Barbara took his order and hustled back to the bar.

"What do you think, 'Mad Dog'? You think we can make a steel hand out of you?" Todd poured himself another glass of beer from the pitcher on the table.

After several years in the business, Filer was used to this type of new hand harassment.

"Well I checked and I didn't have any wood splinters at the end of the day."

"Tough guy, huh? Wait till you mash your fingers between steel beams."

"You got me there," Filer admitted and laughed.

Barbara arrived with another round and Filer's bottle of beer. Filer took a ten out of his money clip and put in on her tray, "keep the change darlin'," he told the attractive young woman.

Filer was listening to Chester when he heard a high pitched female voice from the next table ask, "Do you work for Highline?"

Filer looked over his shoulder and saw a sharp-eyed brunette, sitting with a well built young man, giving him a stare. He met her stare. "Are you talking to me?"

The brunette must have decided he did work for Highline without getting an answer and spit out, "Highline is a lousy outfit. My husband put in an application and they didn't hire him. So they're a cheap outfit that doesn't hire local people."

Filer looked at the hands at his table smiling broadly; "I'm just a hand. I don't work in the front office. But I'll guess maybe your husband wasn't in the right place at the right time."

"My husband could outwork any of Highline's hands any day," the woman continued on in a drunken snit. Then, in a moment to near sobriety she said, "Highline isn't making any friends by not hiring local people. That will come back at them."

Todd looked at the woman and then at Filer waiting for him to defend the company and have the last word.

Filer took up the challenge, "When you go home tonight just don't turn on your lights and see how bad that hurts Highline."

The drunken woman snapped upright in her chair, "Harry, are you going to let him talk to me like that?"

The young man stared past his wife at Filer like a bull that just had a red flag waved at it.

The Highline crew looked at Filer to see how 'Mad Dog' Wilson would handle this amusing, but potentially dangerous situation.

Filer returned the angry man's stare and said, "Pard, you don't want to draw on me. See all of these hands here, they're all Highline hands and they've been working steel all day and they're just looking for someone to take apart."

Filer's short speech shocked the woman's husband out of his angry stance. He grabbed his drunken wife's shoulder so she turned to look at him.

"Shut the fuck up Raelyne. Let's get out of here before you get me killed."

Harry took Raelyne's hand and pulled her across the dance floor to the bar's back door exit.

Todd laughed, "Good one 'Mad Dog'. That's the smartest move that ole boy ever made."

"I'll bet they have great make-up sex when they get home; if she doesn't pass out first," Chester offered.

Parker scooted his chair to the next table and passed the incident around to the Highline hands seated there; and before the band finished playing their number, all of the Highline hands in the bar knew how Filer 'Mad Dog' Wilson had handled the drunken wife who wanted her husband hired by Highline, or killed whichever came first.

For the rest of the evening Filer 'Mad Dog' Wilson didn't have to buy a beer. He met men whose names he would be lucky to remember the next day.

CHAPTER 27

When some of the younger linemen were getting a second wind, Filer announced he was leaving. He'd have a hangover, but he still had enough time to get five or six hours sleep.

"I'll see you in the morning," he promised the hands sitting at his table.

On the way home he figured he hadn't done too badly. The hands would be telling the story about the woman who almost got her husband killed. He smiled when he thought he'd lived up to his nickname.

Filer pulled into the trailer park and parked beside his trailer. He put his key to his front door and saw a flash of furry motion dart under the front of his trailer. From past experience he reckoned it could be a skunk or a raccoon. Which ever animal it turned out to be he wasn't looking forward to seeing the animal again.

CHAPTER 28

In La Rouge, Saskatchewan Cherie Bon Temp banged her beer glass on the bar where she sat with her bikers, the Bonnie Femmes.

"Mon Chers, it's time to make another visit to our business in cowboy land."

A woman, named Tawyna, wearing a leather vest sitting next to Cherie observed, "You work too hard Cher."

Cherie Bon Temp had a following of fifteen to twenty depending on who was pregnant at any given time. The road trip Cherie proposed would take eight days.

Cherie remarked to Tawyna, "There will be many places to drink and get laid on this trip, eh."

Tawyna clinked her beer glass to Cherie's and replied, "Oui."

CHAPTER 29

Coming out his trailer door in the morning Filer saw that the furry animal from the night before was a bedraggled Siamese cat. It peered out at Filer from beneath the trailer as he left the court behind on his way to the show up site.

Filer arrived at the show-up area ready to work. Todd motioned Filer to his company pickup. Chester, Parker and Filer loaded into the truck and left for the next tower site.

"'Mad Dog', you're going to be building a cage today. Once you get a chance to do a cage and arms you can go back to building dog legs. Sounds right doesn't it, 'Mad Dog' building dog legs."

"Seifert told me I'd get a chance work on a wire crew."

"You'll get your chance," Todd added with a hurt tone. "You know it won't hurt you to know how a tower gets built."

"Can't wait to get your feet off the ground, huh 'Mad Dog'," Chester joked. "Stick with us for a while and you'll remember all those times you burned poles."

"Sorry Chester, I like the view from up top."

Parker said, "Are we there yet?"

Todd pulled the pickup into a new site. Two other crews had already arrived and were studying the bundles of steel left at the site.

"Okay gentlemen, let's get out there and shake out some steel," Todd turned his crew loose on a bundle of steel.

"Filer, you help Parker and Chester and I'll work the dog leg."

"Sorry about that 'Mad Dog'," Chester said, "watch out for Parker-he likes men."

"Hold up," Filer said, "maybe you two need some alone time."

Chester and Parker laughed and they all started shaking out the steel, separating the steel parts needed for the cage and arms.

When Filer and Parker had numbered pieces of steel laid out and paired up, Filer used his new best friend, the spud wrench, to align bolt holes so the pieces could be bolted together loosely. Filer was learning it was best to have some leeway in a structure before they started bolting everything down tight.

"You're picking this up real well," Parker complimented Filer. He continued by saying, "We should be through here by early afternoon and moving on to the next site. The stacking crews are working at the site we finished yesterday. We have to keep moving to keep ahead of them.

"S.O.S.," Filer said, "Go fast or you won't last."

Then he asked, "What happens if they catch up to us?"

"That's not going to happen," Parker answered. "We've got a good crew here and that's not going to happen."

"Alright then," Filer said.

Parker asked about the Farewell Bend job, "Is it true most of your crew went to jail after the job was finished?"

"Half of the crew went to jail or prison. But they were all ground men and not linemen," Filer defended his profession, even though he knew he didn't have to.

At eleven thirty the assembly crew heard a rumbling sound coming up the dirt road. Filer had heard the distinctive sound before. It was the engine noise of choppers.

Parker saw Filer look up, "That must be the local farmers."

"Who," Filer asked.

"You know a biker gang. They're probably on their way up here to check on a marijuana patch."

"I didn't figure they were coming up here for a picnic."

The rumbling, spitting noise of choppers disrupted the still mountain air as the bikers came closer. Then the leather clad bikers were roaring past the site without paying any attention to the crew.

When the first of the bikers rolled past the site, the crew noticed more long hair on the riders than would normally be the case, even for bikers. By the time the last chopper passed the tower, several hands wolf-whistled at the female bikers.

Todd stopped moving steel and called the lunch break.

The crew retrieved lunches from the pickup and found places to sit around the site. Todd ended up next to Filer. "How about that 'Mad Dog'? We could have added a rumble in the marijuana jungle with some female bikers to your resume."

"That wasn't in the job description. I'll leave that action to the Forest Service or Fish and Game."

Todd got serious, "If anyone comes after them, it'll be the FBI or D.E.A. The Forest Service or Fish and Game won't make a move without calling in big brother. Anyway, as far as I know we've never had any trouble with them. Just be careful where you go to take a crap."

After lunch, Parker's estimate of the time needed to completely assemble sections of a tower, leaving it ready to be stacked, was on the money. Two hours after the assembly crew finished lunch and then bolted the last bolt on the tower they loaded into the crew pickup and drove for thirty minutes to the next site. There they started shaking out bundles of steel. At the end of the day the crew had assembled most of a second tower.

On the way back to Deer Lodge, Todd asked Filer if he was ready for more night life.

"I'm going to take a pass on this one. I want to call my wife, and then get stocked up with groceries so I can put together a decent lunch.

"You're going to leave me to run the young ones, huh?"

"I've been there man, and I know you wouldn't do it unless you wanted to."

"You could be right," Todd said and smiled.

For the rest of the ride back to Deer Lodge the men in Todd's truck were quiet as if lost in deep thought of the evening to come.

Chapter 30

Harold reflected on his marriage to Leslie. They'd had a good run until he couldn't take Leslie's compulsive shopping and spending any longer. At first, when he could stay at home with Leslie, things went well. But things fell apart when Leslie was home alone. She figured if Harold could have his groupies on the road she could have a lover too. And if her lover was a loser she could spend Harold's money on a loser.

Harold wasn't exactly a model of budgeting virtue, but he managed to put a little money away for hard times. Before he'd met Leslie he had learned to put a little money away for times when he couldn't find any gigs for the band.

Getting the divorce had ended Rip-It-Up's relationship with Leslie in a bad way, so now he needed to be careful about what Leslie would get as part of the divorce settlement. It was bad enough she had almost put him in the poor house while they were married. For her to get half of everything, and his emergency funds was unacceptable. His hold-out fund was now stashed in a money belt in his hotel room. The money belt held thirty thousand dollars he'd worked hard to keep out of Leslie's hands and he didn't intend to lose it to her after getting her out of this life for good.

After Rip-It-Up divorced Leslie he started paying closer attention to the women in his audiences. If he saw a woman smiling his way and keeping time to the music he'd take a chance she would be available after the last set. Harold Roberts didn't intend to let any chances for female companionship slip away.

Soon after he arrived in Deer Lodge Harold saw a petit woman looking his way with a smile. Seated with several biker type females she laughed when he nodded at her, and between sets he bought her a whiskey and introduced himself.

My name is Rip-It-Up," the long-haired musician said over the crowd noise.

"Bien sur," the female replied.

Harold looked puzzled.

"Of course," the female explained, "you are the band leader. You introduced yourself before you started playing."

"That's right," Harold laughed. "What's your name?"

"Je m'appelle Cherie Bon Temp."

Harold shrugged his shoulders.

"My name is Cherie Bon Temp."

In a French accent, that fascinated Harold, Cherie told him she was in Montana to check on her farm. Harold had enough sense not to ask her what she was growing on her farm.

After his last set, with Leslie definitely out of his life, Harold and Cherie became close friends.

Chapter 31

Filer stopped at a supermarket on the way to his trailer. He bought the usual cold cuts, chips, and sodas to make a lunch. At the last minute he detoured to the pet food aisle and picked up some cans of cat food.

A female checker named Cynthia gave Filer a nice smile while she checked his groceries. Filer smile back, but went light on the Filer charm. He was a married man even if he was away from home.

Five minutes later he drove into the trailer court. With an arm full of groceries he opened his trailer and started to go in when he saw a flash of fur still under his trailer.

Be patient kitty. Let me put my groceries away and I'll open you a nice can of cat food."

With the cold cuts in the fridge and chips in the cupboard, Filer opened the cat food and placed it where the animal could eat without feeling threatened.

Watching Filer with a wary eye, the female cat edged up to the cat food and snatched a couple of bites before it got nervous and ran back further under the trailer. Its previous owner had abandoned it after the animal had given her three years of unquestioned affection.

"It's okay Kitty, I'm not going to hurt you," Filer whispered to the stray. "Kitty isn't right," Filer searched for a name for the cat and a name came to him, "Girlfriend, I'm going to call you Girlfriend. If someone asks me why, I'll tell them that's the first name that came to mind when I picked your name."

Filer reached to pet Girlfriend and she disappeared in the shadows under the trailer.

"Okay then, later Girlfriend."

CHAPTER 32

Kylie had a boy friend. She didn't take him home because Abbey didn't like him. Her mother was polite to Gil, but Kylie knew when her mother was just being polite.

Gil Hooks thought of himself as a stud. How he got that idea would be hard to understand. He didn't have a job, and he still sneaked in and out of his parents' house.

Gil had good looks, but he was beginning to put on weight from lack of exercise and drinking too many six packs with his buds.

Kylie liked him because Gil reminded her of a young 'Mad Dog'. She saw, in Gil, a show that wasn't backed up by substance, unlike her father who backed up everything he said or did with personal responsibility.

"Can you loan me ten dollars until next week?" Gil pleaded with Kylie.

"What do you need ten dollars for?" Kylie knew he'd spend the ten on beer so he could impress his buds. "I wouldn't mind loaning you the money if I knew you'd pay it back."

"If you're going to whine about it, forget it," Gil broke eye contact with Kylie.

"You know I work at Sears everyday, putting in eight hours a day. If I can keep a job, you should be able to at least get some kind of work."

"I work," Gil said stubbornly.

"You mean at the car wash. They fired you two weeks ago."

Kylie laid out a plan for Gil, "I'll loan you ten dollars if you spend some of it taking me to a movie."

Gil frowned; he needed the ten to go out with his friends.

Kylie took ten dollars out of her purse and held it out to Gil. She considered it the price of keeping a boyfriend. "Come by and pick me up after work. I need a ride home."

She'd given Gil her bus money.

"You got it girl," Gil promised putting the ten in his pocket.

Kylie knew he was just as likely to forget to pick her up as not.

Chapter 33

An orange sun rose over Deer Lodge-another beautiful day in paradise. Filer woke up a little sorer than usual. After humping steel for the last couple of weeks all his muscles ached. "I'd better get used to it," Filer admonished himself. "It's not going to get any easier from here on. And I hope it doesn't get much worse."

After a quick shower, Filer put on a T-shirt and jeans and pulled on a Carhart long sleeve shirt for the early morning chill. He laced up the high top whites and grabbed his cooler filled with sandwiches and a thermos of black coffee for lunch.

As he opened the trailer door, Filer saw the dejected bundle of fur peaking out from beneath the trailer. Taking a few minutes Filer returned to the trailer kitchen and opened a can of cat food. He replaced an empty can of cat food with a fresh can and watched over his shoulder as the stray, now called Girlfriend came shyly to the can and started eating. Having done his good deed, he walked over the bridge and up the road to the show-up site.

CHAPTER 34

Filer finished the walk from his trailer to the show-up site. The weather in the flat land was holding up, hot and dry. Their tower sites above Goldcreek were generally a little cooler. It was worth the rough ride getting there to avoid the heat around Garrison.

Filer joined the crew gathering parts under Todd's direction.

"Okay fellers, let's go build some towers," Todd cheered his crew on.

Once his crew was aboard the power wagon Todd steered it, bumping over the gravel roads connecting the Forest Service roads and the tower sites.

"You'll be working with Parker again building cages today Filer," Todd said.

"Okay boss," Filer said, then looked at Parker and gave him a thumbs-up.

The power wagon raised a dust cloud as it passed through the many piles of tailings left from when the hills were dredged for gold.

The area reminded Filer of the area around Idaho City, Idaho, which was filled with miles of bare river rock mounds left by Idaho miners.

Todd stopped the power wagon at the summit of a pine covered mountain. According to the over flight Filer had taken with Ozzie and Lucille, he estimated they were one third of the way through the thirty mile stretch of the job.

Although the footing crew had cleared the site of trees the air still reminded Filer of a pine freshener dangling from the company truck's mirror. With the pads in place on the uneven hill side the stacking crew following the assembly crew could raise the assembled tower to fit the site on an even level.

The crew started building and the stillness of the mountain gave way to bundles of steel being shaken out. The sound of their work echoed off the next hillside site that had been cleared by the footing crew and was absorbed by the surrounding forest.

Before the different steel pieces became a tower they looked somewhat fragile. The pickup sticks quality of the steel bundles was transformed into the different elements of the tower. Each of these elements being assembled would later be stacked into a tower unit. For the time being the assembly crews worked steadily matching numbered pieces, using spud wrenches to line up bolt holes and loosely bolting the pieces together. X-braces joined legs, and a cage came together to fit onto a body.

Parker picked up sun baked steel pieces and laid the pieces out to be bolted together.

"You haven't been at the 'Arrow' for a while," he accused Filer.

"I didn't know it was a part of the job," Filer answered as he worked his part of the cage.

"You know what I mean," Parker insisted.

"I guess I don't know what you mean," Filer said obstinately.

Parker didn't want to admit they wanted Filer as part of the after work group, so he said, "We put you on a tab, and you owe us a couple pitchers of beer."

Filer smiled, "So that's how it works."

The first cage they were working on took shape under a perfect blue sky. With the cage completed the pair started shaking out the next bundle.

"You know, there are only so many stories with the guys on this crew. It can get boring without new blood," Parker said.

"I know what you mean," Filer said as he reflected on the jobs he'd done in the past.

The pair worked in silence for some minutes, and then Parker said, "Do you have a family 'Mad Dog'?"

"I…" Filer started an answer.

"I have an ex," Parker spat out, "The bitch got everything. We were together for fifteen years and she treated me like a stranger at the end. The really bad thing is-she did her homework and cleaned me out."

Before the end of the day Filer had reluctantly learned all about Parker's problems with his ex. It would take a little longer to find out Parker had cheated on her several times; and when his wife had enough, she left him. It amazed Filer that Parker couldn't see why his wife decided she would be better off without him. It was just as clear to him that Parker missed being married to 'The Bitch' as he always called her.

CHAPTER 35

In Oregon, Leslie had passed the last point of no return. Harold's alimony check was late. Now she'd have to put off her shopping trip to Portland. She'd planned to meet her next affair.

Instead of a shopping trip to Portland, Leslie got in the convertible she'd insisted Harold buy for her and drove to a sleazy bar on the outskirts of Portland where Harold used to have a steady gig. She was well known in the bar and she thought she could find a man to buy her a drink or two.

Chapter 36

Filer called Abbey and updated her on what he'd been doing on the job, and then expanded on the extra job for Shane McLane.

"I guess I didn't really hear you before," Abbey said, "You and Ozzie are going to build a power line for Shane McLane, the movie star," Abbey stated in disbelief.

"That's what it looks like," Filer confirmed.

"We saw one of his pictures together. I think it was *Kill or be Killed*, or something like that. Did you meet Shane?"

"Ozzie, Trina and I had dinner with the man in Ozzie's R.V. Actually the man wants to go up some poles with me," Filer bragged a little.

"What is he like?" Abbey wanted to know.

"Well, he wasn't too happy when I didn't recognize him right away. Ozzie finally told me he was a movie star. Then it came to me that we went to one of his pictures together. I didn't tell him I fell asleep in the middle of the picture. He looked a lot happier after I told him about seeing one of his pictures."

"Have you seen his cabin?"

"I've only seen the outside of the cabin so far. It is a lot more cabin than most have in this part of the country."

"How long will it take you to build the power line?"

"Once we get the go-ahead it'll probably take a month of working part time to finish the job."

Abbey had a thought, "Filer, Kylie would love it if you got an autograph from Shane McLane."

"We'll see," Filer replied, not sounding too enthusiastic.

Filer and Abbey talked about being together over the Labor Day weekend and then Filer told Abbey he loved her and said good-bye.

It was still early evening when Filer got off the phone with Abbey, so he decided to take a walk in the Garrison trailer Park. Walking wasn't his usual habit, but he told himself he needed the exercise, in order to get a good night's sleep.

A gravel trail wound through the trailer court. Each trailer had just enough grass lawn to make the trailer court homey. Filer walked the gravel pathway for the first time, not knowing where it would take him.

Cottonwood trees, along the path, rustled with a low breeze; and he could hear the nearby stream flowing over the rocks and boulders in the stream bed. Someone in the trailer park had a wood fire burning, and Filer could smell wood smoke filling the air. Filer thought he'd picked a good one for an evening walk.

Turning a corner at the far end of the path, Filer saw a picnic table filled with people. It looked like two families were sharing the table. Filer stopped before continuing past the table; then noticed one of the big men at the table motioning him over.

Filer hesitated for a minute, making up his mind if he should get involved. While he waited, the people at the table continued talking and laughing. The whole scene reminded him of the good times he'd had when the Wilson family had had gatherings. The big man, who had first waved, waved again and smiled.

"Okay," Filer thought, "it's time to make some new friends."

The big man, who had waved at him and the woman sitting beside him, scooted together on the bench, making room for Filer at the end. Filer was soon chatting with Mary and Stan Walton, when they could be heard over their three young boys. Filer also met Steve and Bret Bakerson.

During the round of introductions, Filer learned the big men were mechanics for Highline Electrical Construction.

Steve eyed Filer and said, "We've heard about you 'Mad Dog'."

Filer cocked an eyebrow.

"Ozzie Harper told us about the Farewell Bend, Oregon pole job. He said you're a hero for keeping a pregnant woman from being electrocuted; and he's had a few free beers, entertaining us with tall tales about the copper thieves on your crew who got arrested."

"Don't forget about the murderer 'Mad Dog' threatened to come after like a junk yard dog," Stan Walton added, chuckling.

"Oh yeah, Ozzie also said you adopted a stray cat here in Deer Lodge, and named her Girlfriend. How's that working out for you 'Mad Dog'?"

Filer didn't let the kidding get under his skin, and replied, "Girlfriend is real good company. She keeps me sane. I might have to kill anyone who messes with Girlfriend."

The conversation continued with more drinks poured out of a frosty pitcher. The two married couples talked about their pets, and how pets become a part of the family.

At the end of his second Tequila Daiquiri, and just before he was going to make his excuse for leaving, Filer connected with a thought that had been rattling around in the back of his mind. With the thought firmly in mind he tipped his glass to his hosts and said, "I know you two. You're 'Black Bart' and 'White Lightning'. I just don't know who's who."

The two big men smiled at one another, and Steve said, "How'd you figure that out?"

Filer replied with a knowing smile, "Someone breaks down at a tower site and they call for 'Black Bart' or 'White Lightning.' It's a small world."

"Well," Stan explained, "I'm 'White Lightning' and Steve is 'Black Bart'. Sometime when we've got a little more time, and we're a little drunker, we'll tell you how we got the nicknames."

Before Filer could leave, Bret Bakerson invited him to have a slice of huckleberry pie. Filer nodded yes, and Bret cut a slice of dark blue huckleberry pie rimmed in whipped cream and set it in front of him with a plastic fork.

Filer didn't know what to expect when he took a bite. The bite of pie melted in his mouth.

"That's the best pie I've had since I got here in Deer Lodge," Filer complimented Bret.

"Tell that to Steve. Steve baked the pie. If you stay on his good side you'll find out he's a fine cook."

Filer didn't know what to say, so he concentrated on finishing the slice of pie on his plate.

The conversation started to wind down when the mosquitoes started biting, and the setting sun turned the horizon red against the cloudless blue sky. Bret asked Filer if he wanted the last slice of pie to take home. Filer accepted the slice and nodded at Steve.

During the next years, while Filer worked for Highline Electrical Construction, he stopped by the mechanics shop to drink a beer or two with Steve 'Black Bart' Bakerson, also sometimes known as 'Cookie', and Stan 'White Lightning' Walton whenever he needed time off from the line hands. He appreciated their friendship, and the sense of companionship he missed because of the early passing of Clayton Wilson.

CHAPTER 37

The next morning, after a good night's sleep, Filer left Girlfriend in his trailer, locked the trailer door and started an early morning walk to the show up site. Walking to the site he shuffled through loose gravel at the side of the pavement. The short walk reminded him of walking to the bus stop before school as a kid. He didn't have this kind of memories often, but the early morning hour under a clear blue sky, and the expectation of catching a ride to work brought back reminiscences of living in Riverview along the Snake River in Idaho. It had been a good time except for the school experience. He hadn't been overly fond of school, sitting at a desk all day, half listening to some teacher make mountains out of mole hills. All they had to teach over the years could be summed up in a sentence or two-keep your mouth shut and do what you're told. The second sentence would vary according to the subject they were teaching. He had listened enough to graduate from high school and attend heavy equipment school. Now he was very proud that everything he knew about line work, he'd learned on his own without sitting behind a desk. And, he thought, the most important lessons could only be learned by experience.

Inside the show up site, Filer walked through the different areas to where Todd waited in the assembly section. Filer spotted Todd's truck.

Todd spoke to Filer, "Seifert wants you to work erection. He's satisfied you know enough about assembly to move on."

Filer didn't look surprised. His progress with Highline was going according to the deal he'd made with Seifert. He just hoped the man intended to keep his word about him ending up on a wire crew.

Todd said, "I'm supposed to hand you over to Rondo Dance. Rondo's the foreman of the erection crew you'll be working with. And guess what, your old buddy Ozzie will be there running the crane."

Again Filer didn't seem surprised; so Todd motioned for Filer to get into the truck. Once Filer was aboard Todd drove around the show up area until he spotted the erection crew foreman's pickup. "Well old buddy," Todd said, "It was nice working with you. And don't forget our little adventure at Fred's. Maybe we'll get a chance to go again some time." Todd held out his hand to Filer and Filer smiled when he shook Todd's hand.

Todd pulled his truck opposite Rondo's vehicle and rolled down his window. "I've got Filer Wilson here and he's just dying to get a little erection time."

Filer exited Todd's truck and waited as Todd pulled away; then he walked the short distance to stand facing Rondo Dance.

"So you're Filer "Mad Dog" Wilson. You better get in."

Filer got into Rondo's truck and waited for the usual question about ex cons and copper thieves.

"My guys are out getting bolts. We'll be heading for the site in fifteen or twenty minutes," Rondo paused as if searching for something else to say. After a minute or so the dark skinned man who could be a Native American or a Mexican broke his silence, "What do you want me to call you?"

"Filer, 'Mad Dog', or Wilson; most of the hands on this job call me 'Mad Dog'," Filer concluded. Now he felt a little uncomfortable with the man after his question.

"Well then, Filer "Mad Dog" Wilson, I guess Mr. Wilson is out of the question," Rondo broke into a big smile and laughed.

Tension in the truck cab eased; and then the rest of Rondo's crew arrived and filled the truck bed with boxes of bolts.

With everyone loaded into his pickup Rondo pulled out of the show up area and headed for the Highline tower site. A second truck with three other men on the crew, Pete, Kurk and Jack, followed Rondo out of the show up area.

Rondo used the time on route to introduce his crew. Filer met Frank, Matt, and Dean. Of the four men Frank and Dean were married. Matt was divorced and Rondo was single. Two of the men were linemen apprentices waiting to get on wire crews, and the other two, Rondo and Dean, were construction types happy enough to be on permanent erection duty.

When the hour ride to the erection site was over the erection crew also knew Filer was married, had a daughter, and was a journeyman lineman. This meant Filer would be next up to go on a wire crew if an opening happened.

"Here we are boys. Save the B.S. for after work, we've got a tower to stack."

Rondo gave the crew their assignments, "Filer, you'll be with Dean, Frank and me on the tag lines. Matt, Jack and Kurk, you'll be on the ground. Pete, you'll be with Ozzie."

For Filer's benefit Rondo explained further, "We'll have a man on the leg ready to guide it onto the foundation splice plates." Rondo added, "You have to be damn careful and watch what you're doing. It's too easy to end up with mashed or missing fingers."

This wasn't the first or last safety speech Filer would hear. This one was a safety talk that wasn't the result of a safety meeting, so even though it seemed like common sense to Filer he figured Rondo's words came from legitimate concern for crew safety.

"Okay boss, I hear you," Filer responded.

Dean spoke to Filer when Rondo finished his speech, "Are you the guy who turned in the murderer on your crew?"

Filer shook his head as they waited for Ozzie to arrive, "A ground man that worked for me on a pole job in Oregon was arrested for murdering a woman. She sold drugs and he stole her stash and shot her with her own shotgun. But I didn't know any of this until I read it in the papers. He did his job and wasn't much more of an asshole than anyone else on the crew."

"So you didn't get a big reward?"

"You know, I don't know where people come up with this stuff. No, I didn't get a penny. I was lucky they didn't charge me with stealing copper."

Frank and Matt were listening closely to the conversation and Filer hoped he wouldn't have to tell the story over again.

As his story ended Ozzie arrived in his dually. Ozzie parked his pickup and came to the leg where the erection crew was standing.

"Hey there Rondo, I see you've got 'Mad Dog' here. Be careful, things can get a little exciting with 'Mad Dog' around." Ozzie grinned at 'Mad Dog' and said, "Let's get his tower up." Ozzie patted Rondo on the shoulder and started toward his crane with Pete in tow. The crane was sitting in a strategic position among the tower parts. From where it sat Ozzie could pick up all the sections of the tower.

With the stacking crew ready, Ozzie maneuvered his crane over each leg. Pete hooked the crane cable up to a leg and the linemen used tag lines to settle the legs into splice plates. Then the linemen bolted the leg onto the foundation. One leg followed another until all of the legs were loosely bolted into place to provide a level platform for addition of the body.

Filer, Dean, Frank and Rondo each had a tag line on the four corners of the body guiding it onto the legs. With full bolt bags provided by the ground men, they started in loosely bolting the body to the legs. Matt, Jack and Kurk worked the ground filling bolt bags for the men above.

The scattered elements of the tower sites were organized by the linemen into an in-line tower. A cage with arms topped by a bridge followed the legs and body as the linemen worked their way from the foundation upward.

At the end of his first day working on the erection crew, Filer was impressed by how well they worked together.

CHAPTER 38

On a Monday morning Wire Superintendent Thomas Bradford studied paperwork on his desk. A wire crew foreman had an emergency at home and he hoped he could promote Filer Wilson to foreman. He'd heard good things from General Superintendent Seifert about Filer and now he wanted Filer to replace the lineman on emergency leave.

With Seifert's recommendation in mind Bradford was confident that Filer could handle the job if he was willing.

Filer had worked erection for a week when Rondo told him to report to Wire Superintendent Bradford's office. Now he sat in front of Bradford's desk.

"Don Seifert tells me you're a good hand. And I asked your assembly and erection foremen what they thought."

Filer watched the wire superintendent shift in his chair. The Wire Superintendent then continued, "Both of them said I could trust you with a crew. Of course they don't know how good you are working wire so I called P.G. & E. P.G. & E. recommended you. They even threw in a good word on your work during the Portland ice storm. So, Mr. Wilson, it looks like you're our new wire crew foreman."

During all of this Filer hadn't said anything.

"If you want the promotion fill out this form and get yourself a company rig and a gas card. Meet me at the show up site tomorrow morning and I'll introduce you to your crew-any questions?"

Filer accepted the form, filled it out and returned it to Bradford.

CHAPTER 39

Driving through the Highline Electric show up site Filer passed the assembly, and erection areas. The dusty show up site resembled the staging area for a caravan. Once a day it filled with swarms of men moving among the many piles of bolts, rope, cribbing, hoists, shoes and socks, bicycles and other materials to collect the parts necessary to assemble, erect and string the large reels of aluminum wire that would eventually conduct electricity from tower to tower over the thirty mile stretch of sites now under construction.

Parking in the wire section of the show up area, Filer waited for the Wire Superintendent to arrive. He'd been waiting ten minutes when Thomas Bradford arrived. He had three men with him in his crew cab. Bradford parked his vehicle next to Filer's truck and got out of his truck. The three men with Bradford also exited his vehicle and they all walked to Filer's company flatbed truck. It was an awkward moment for them. Then Bradford said, "Here's your crew, you'll be the foreman."

One of the men named Jimmy Glenn didn't look too happy to be working for the new foreman. The other men, Tony Blaine, and Greg Mac Gregor shook hands with Filer. With introductions completed Bradford got back in his truck and handed Filer a metal clipboard with the job specs, and said, "If you need anything let me know."

It wasn't the first time Filer had the feeling the world, or at least a little part of the world had fallen on him.

Jimmy Glenn smirked at the other men and waited for Filer to give his first orders.

Filer ignored Jimmy and looked at the schedule Bradford left with him. He took his time and when he looked up, he said, "Okay we've got travelers to hang, let's get busy.

On the way to the first site, Filer laid out how they would work the tower.

Jimmy, you'll be working on the structure with me. Tony, you and Greg will be on the ground."

Filer knew it would be a contest the first couple of days working with Jimmy. He also knew if Jimmy had it in him to be a boss Bradford would have put him in-charge, and he hadn't.

Once they arrived on site, the crew split up as Filer had outlined. Filer and Jimmy climbed the tower and got in position to bring up the ladder they would be working on.

As the two men worked off of a ladder hanging from a tower arm, Jimmy steadied travelers as Filer maneuvered them into place and locked them down. When Filer gestured at Jimmy for slack, Jimmy glared at him like a rookie. So it went for their first day working together.

Tony and Greg worked well on the ground.

By the end of the first day, despite their personal differences, Filer had led his new crew to complete work on two towers. "Not bad for my first day as boss," he congratulated himself. And he continued thinking, "No one injured or killed."

When the crew crowded into the company truck for the ride back to Garrison, a normal end of day trip would be a chance for the crew to debrief with tall tales and kidding about the day's work. Because of Jimmy's soreness of being passed over for the foreman's position, the cab full of men rode in silence.

Just outside the show-up site Filer knew he'd have to offer his new crew an invitation to beers at the Broken Arrow.

"Well boys, I'm buying at the Broken Arrow. I'll see you there." Filer said, making it a point to look at Jimmy; although he guessed Jimmy might show up and continue his silent bit. That would be fine with him.

Bradford was waiting at the show-up area and asked Filer how the day's work had gone.

Filer said, "We finished two towers and no one's hurt. No accidents," Filer replied.

Bradford smiled, "Yeah, you had a good day." He continued by saying, "Look, I know Jimmy's a little sore because I didn't use him as a foreman. He's a good hand, but he needs more experience before I can trust him as a foreman. You should take it as a compliment that you're the man I picked as the foreman. Some men can be damn good working the steel and wire, but they'll never be in-charge because they don't have the instinct for working men. You've got that instinct Filer. I know Jimmy will come around. Help him if you can. You might make a friend for life." Bradford patted Filer on the shoulder and finished his pep talk by saying, "'A good day's work for a good day's pay', huh 'Mad Dog'."

Chapter 40

"Invited me to drink some beers," Jimmy thought harshly. "I can buy my own beers and I could have run that crew." Still, Jimmy Glenn cleaned up and got ready to drive into the Broken Arrow. He showered and put on clean and ironed Levis and a western shirt. He had a pair of cowboy boots and a new Stetson hat. He liked the cowboy image. "I'll bet Filer "Mad Dog" Wilson doesn't have a nice pair of boots like these," Jimmy said to himself and smiled.

CHAPTER 41

Filer sat in the Broken Arrow nursing a long neck Budweiser watching his new crew suck down a couple of pitchers of beer. He studied each man. Tony and Greg drank their beers and listened to Rip-It-Up and the Misfits performing on stage. Jimmy Glenn hadn't shown up yet, but Filer knew he'd come. Jimmy wasn't the type to pass up free beers.

On cue Jimmy came into the bar wearing a full cowboy get up. "I've got you now; you're nickname is Cowboy."

Among the regulars at the 'Arrow' Jimmy hardly stood out. Most of the linemen and construction workers on the footing crews left their work clothes at home after work and replaced them with Stetsons or do-rags. A few of the townies who refused to give the 'Arrow' up to the linemen and footing crews, sat apart, drinking and listening to Rip-It-Up and the Misfits playing their version of Rock and Roll.

Adding to the mix, honest to God bikers from Missoula occasionally stopped in the 'Arrow' on their way to Bozeman. Generally the different groups maintained a truce in the bar.

Jimmy Glenn found his way to Filer's table, pulled up a chair and sat down. Filer signaled to a passing cocktail waitress and ordered another pitcher of beer for the table.

Filer sipped at his beer pacing himself. He wanted to be ready to lead the crew in the morning. Before long, as he sat with the crew, someone asked him to retell the Farewell Bend, Oregon story.

"I'll tell you that one another time," Filer promised, "if you want a good story, I'll tell you about the Portland ice storm. I worked two weeks straight, sixteen hours a day, without a change of clothes."

No one told him to stop, so Filer launched into his ice storm story.

"I was working out of the 17th street P.G. & E. in January 1980. When Abbey, my wife, got up it had already snowed an inch. One inch of snow on the ground around Portland is like having a foot of snow in Idaho where I grew-up. Abbey made breakfast for me and Kylie, my daughter.

I decided to leave for work a little early because of the snow. A little snow on the Interstate and Oregon drivers will end up in sliding fender benders. They can't drive in snow. It's a steep learning curve and it doesn't snow enough for those people to get ahead of the curve.

On the way into the 17th street show up site I passed five or six slide and kiss accidents. I was right to leave early because it took me the extra half hour just to get there on time.

When I got to the yard, our foreman explained two hundred thousand people were without power and we wouldn't be going home until we'd returned power to as many homes as we could get to.

We were working in four man crews. The company sent out every service truck available and they still didn't have enough trucks or crews to cover the parts of the city affected by the ice storm.

Filer stole a sip of beer and then continued, "Now pay attention. An ice storm happens when it snows, thaws enough to get a layer of water and then freezes overnight. You've all seen those pretty pictures of trees covered in ice. The weight of the ice on power lines pulls the power lines down between poles and away from homes.

We finished one job of running a line from a transformer to a house and were working on a job across the street, when a tree fell over from the weight of the ice on it and tore the line we'd just repaired down.

An ice storm only happens once every five years or so, so the company definitely wasn't prepared to handle all the damage. They put us up in hotel rooms, but we only got eight hours off in every twenty-four hours.

The company made sure we had one hot meal per day and we could pick up sandwiches at anytime. That didn't make it any warmer working outdoors. We were cold and miserable most of the time," Filer stopped and took another drink of beer, "but people were offering us coffee and hot chocolate, and inviting us to come into their homes to warm up once their power was restored.

One old guy invited our crew into his house and served us hot coffee. He had cooked the coffee over a wood fire in his fireplace and was patiently waiting for us to get his electricity back on line. While we drank his coffee he had a little philosophy to pass on. 'You young men probably don't remember cooking on a wood stove. It's only been fifty or sixty years ago that most people still heated their homes with coal and cooked on wood burning stoves.' Being the ice storm was in 1980, he was talking about the 1920's which would make what he was telling us pretty close to right. And, around that time a lot of people weren't hooked up to an electrical grid.

The old guy continued to philosophize, 'In my early years a lot of folks still rode in horse drawn buggies.' The old man offered us more coffee. He was enjoying the company. 'If you need to warm up again just come back and I'll have more coffee for you.'

'Come on guys, finish your coffee,' our foreman said and thanked the old guy. 'Thanks for the hot coffee and the hospitality. Your power will be back on in twenty or thirty minutes.'

'Thank you boys; I hope the rest of your day goes well.'

"He wasn't the only one to invite us in, once their power came back on people wanted to be helpful.

We'd been working for a week and it hadn't gotten any warmer. We were still working sixteen hour days, but a few people thought we should be working faster. All we could do was to keep on working the power lines.

We were working on getting an old folks home back on line and had blocked off one end of a street with our service vehicle. We didn't know another crew had blocked off the other end of the street.

A woman wearing an expensive winter outfit came up to me. I was working the ground. She didn't look too happy and she had a question for me."

'Young man, do you know you have my home blocked off. I can't get to my house.'

"I didn't say anything," and she said, 'What are you going to do about my house being blocked off?'

"We should have this job done in half an hour. Then we'll move our truck and you can get to your house."

'What am I supposed to do for half an hour?'

"Maybe the woman thought whining a little would help and said," 'I don't know what I'm going to do because you're blocking me from getting home.'

"Look," I said, "you can wait for half an hour and then we'll be out of the way."

'Well, I don't want to wait, so what am I supposed to do?'

"I'd been working straight for sixteen hours and I didn't want to play games with this woman. Next thing I knew I was telling her, "Well lady it looks to me like the only way out is for you to commit suicide."

"I know I could have been more patient with this woman, but she hadn't been working double shifts, and she could have parked her car and walked half a block."

Filer saw Jimmy shake his head and asked him what was on his mind.

"What if the woman had three or four bags of groceries she wanted to unload? Did you think of that?"

Filer shook his head and admitted he hadn't thought of that at the time. "You're right Cowboy. I didn't think of that at the time."

Despite having been called Cowboy, Jimmy smiled, chalking up a point in his favor against his new boss.

"Anyway," Filer said, "I didn't hear anything from the bosses, so I guess she didn't complain. Or if she did complain they didn't pass it along.

We kept working for the next week and finally got ahead of the storm. The weather warmed up and the ice storm ended. We worked a lot of overtime and P.G. & E. was happy to pay it."

Filer took a deep breath and finished his story. "The job at Farewell Bend had its moments. The truth is that I didn't know the whole story until I read what happened in the newspapers. I worked a lot harder during the 1980 ice storm than most of the jobs I've done. People were grateful we worked all of those hours getting the job done."

"Well, 'Mad Dog', I hope we don't bore you here on our little steel job," Jimmy offered a snide comment.

"It won't hurt my feelings if the job is boring as long as the pay is on time," Filer said.

Jimmy didn't have a come back comment, so Filer figured he was still in-charge. For the rest of the night the crew drank their beers and talked about their work experiences hoping to impress their new boss.

An hour before closing time, Filer told his crew he was leaving early. His crew declined to follow his good example and decided to hang on until last call for alcohol.

CHAPTER 42

True to her expectations, Gil left Kylie without a ride after work. She'd begged a ride home from work with a co-worker.

"I don't know why you put up with Gil. You're smarter than that aren't you?" Janet Farley said. "It won't get any better you know," she cautioned her friend.

"He has his good points," Kylie defended Gil, thinking of the times he treated her really nice.

"Good points or not, that boy is out with his buds and you're here alone. If it was me I'd be looking for a new, better boy friend."

While Kylie waited at home, Gil was with his buds. They were finishing the last six pack of a case of Coors Gil had provided with Kylie's money when Gil looked at this wristwatch.

"Damn, I was supposed to pick Kylie up after work," Gil exclaimed.

"Hey, she's a big girl," Bo Grant said, "She'll find a way to get home."

The other two members of Gil's crew smiled in drunken agreement.

"You don't understand. You've never seen her old man. Believe me you wouldn't want to get on his bad side. I'm just lucky he's out of town on a line job somewhere in Montana.

Get in the car you guys."

Bo Grant stayed sprawled out, leaning on the park bench.

"Come on Bo," Gil complained when Bo was slow getting into the car. "Get in the fucking car man."

"Okay, okay," Bo grinned. "I can't help it if you're whipped."

Gil glared at Bo in the rear view mirror, "At least I've got a girl. What's your excuse?"

"I could have a girlfriend just like that," Bo said and snapped his fingers"

No one said anything else.

CHAPTER 43

The day after Filer treated his new crew to beers at the Arrow he got to the show up site early and waited for them to arrive.

Tony and Greg drove in in Tony's Camaro. The two men left Tony's vehicle and walked to Filer's flatbed truck. It was an awkward moment for the two and Filer put them at ease by handing them a list of materials he'd written out while waiting for them to arrive. Just after the two men departed on their scavenger hunt Jimmy drove up. After a minute he got out of his Ford truck and walked up to Filer. When he got close Filer saw he had a black eye.

"Hey there Cowboy, looks like you picked up a souvenir last night."

Jimmy stared at Filer like a pissed off teenager and didn't say anything. Once again he'd let his new nickname stand.

When he didn't get any feed back from Jimmy, Filer said, "Tony and Greg are getting travelers. Go ahead and get in the truck."

Jimmy continued his silence while he put his gear in the front seat of the company flatbed.

With all of the material gathered and stowed in the truck, Tony and Greg got in the flatbed cab with Filer and Jimmy. Filer pulled the truck out of the show up area and headed for the work site.

It was a twenty minute ride to the work site and no one was talking. Filer decided Tony and Greg were going to let Jimmy tell his own story of what had happened the evening before. He assumed the men had stayed at the 'Arrow', and anything could have happened.

Filer took the silence as an opportunity to outline the day's work schedule, "We should finish up the first tower before lunch so we have enough time to get set up early on the next tower. I want to eat lunch under the next tower even if we have to work a little past our regular lunch time."

Jimmy said, "We need an early lunch break."

Greg, probably the shiest crew member backed Jimmy up, "Cowboy's right boss, we need an early lunch."

From that moment on the crew used Jimmy's new nickname, and, far from being angry, Jimmy seemed pleased.

As if nothing out of the ordinary had happened the crew looked at Filer to see what he would say about an early lunch.

Filer knew the feeling. He'd had it himself a hundred times before after a long night out drinking.

"I'll tell you what. You guys finish the first tower and I'll give you lunch and a nap on the next hill." He wanted to make a good impression on the Wire Superintendent. The crew didn't say anything, so he assumed they'd agreed to his plan.

At the site, Filer and Jimmy climbed to one arm of the structure leaving Greg and Tony on the ground.

Working the next tower Filer and Jimmy would be on the ground-taking a break and Greg and Tony would work the tower.

"How'd you get that black eye?" Filer asked Jimmy.

If a lineman had been in a good tussle he generally wasn't shy talking about it.

Jimmy seemed to loosen up a bit and started telling Filer his Broken Arrow adventure.

Filer had learned that it was important at this stage to listen instead of talking. He had plenty of hair raising tales of his own to tell, and people generally listened. Now it was his turn to listen. He tuned back into Jimmy's story.

"….and the biker didn't like me talking to Gena, the cocktail waitress, so he decided he'd try me on for size."

Filer was happy he'd decided not to stay at the bar for the extra hour the evening before.

"….and he looks worse than I do." Filer heard the last part of the story as he concentrated on adjusting the last traveler. He relaxed for a minute as he watched Jimmy finish up his job and his story.

The kid might do okay once he forgot about being the meanest rooster in the barn yard.

"How long have you been chasing cocktail waitresses?" He asked Jimmy. He didn't wait for an answer. "You know if you find a woman that's seventy-five percent of what you want, that's probably one hundred percent of what you deserve. Pick yourself a woman and it won't be so important to close the bars down every night. Believe me, it's a lot less wear and tear going home a little early."

Jimmy looked down at the ground below and started down the tower. Filer looked a last time at the travelers they had installed and started down himself. They had finished the job on schedule and he intended to live up to the deal he'd made with the crew.

CHAPTER 44

When Dave gave them the word that Shane wanted to go ahead with the private power line to his cabin, Ozzie and Filer, in an evening after work, surveyed the route from the main power line to Shane's cabin site. After surveying the site Ozzie talked to Rip-It-Up and got him on board as a ground man.

Filer asked Cowboy if he was interested in making a little extra money; and Cowboy surprised him by saying yes. Now all they had to do was wait until they got the go ahead from Dave to start the job.

CHAPTER 45

Filer was relaxing in his easy chair before going to bed when he heard a knock at his door.

Girlfriend jumped down from his lap when he got up to answer the door. Filer came face to face with his past at the open door. Rupert, his ground man, many years ago on the Farewell Bend job stood on his door step.

"Hi Filer," Rupert said, and when Filer continued staring at him in surprise, he asked, "Do you think I could come in?"

"Sure," Filer replied, "You surprised me there for a minute."

Inside, Filer pointed to the small sofa, offering Rupert a place to sit. "What's up my man?" He asked Rupert.

"I'm between jobs," Rupert started explaining. Then he interrupted himself. "Could I have a glass of water?"

"Okay. Do you want a beer?"

"No, water will be fine for right now."

Filer went to the kitchen and filled a glass with water and then offered it to Rupert.

The young man lifted the glass, drank half of it, and then began speaking, "Filer I need a couple of favors."

"Let's start out with one favor and go on from there," Filer said.

"Okay, well I need a place to stay for a couple of days until my last pay check catches up to me."

Filer didn't say no, but he didn't say yes either.

"I'll help out Filer; and I won't get in your way," Rupert produced a half smile. "Hey Filer we can talk about old times."

Filer didn't look convinced.

"I'll pay you a little rent when I get my paycheck."

"You won't be very comfortable. This trailer sleeps two with an uncomfortable fold out bed for a second person."

Rupert looked relieved. "Thanks Filer. I promise I won't be any trouble."

If Filer could have guessed what would come out of Rupert's visit, he later wondered if he'd have been so willing to let Rupert into his life.

Now that Rupert was in, he assumed the uncomfortable role of trailer guest.

While Filer worked Rupert made himself at home, raiding Filer's refrigerator and generally leaving a mess in front of the T.V.

After a day's hard work Filer came home to the trailer park where Rupert started asking questions about the job they had worked together in Ontario, Oregon.

"So did you know Nicole Stickley before she was murdered?"

Filer replied, a little out of patience, "I'll tell you what I tell everyone else. I only know what I read in the newspapers and what I saw on T.V."

Rupert didn't give up and asked, "Did you hear Steve Williams talking about her?"

"No I did not. You would have had more chances to talk to him than I did since you were both ground men on the job."

Rupert slowed down for a minute and said, "Williams and his brother Cliff mostly kept to themselves except when they started planning to hide and steal the copper wire."

Filer asked a question, "If you knew they were planning to steal copper why weren't you arrested?"

"As I told the sheriff, I knew they were saving copper, but I thought it was a company thing," Rupert said and paused a minute. "I never knew about the copper coils they rolled off into the sage brush and later collected to sell at the metal scrape yard."

Chapter 46

Back in Albany, Abbey waited for a call from Filer. Neither of them wrote letters. At times their telephone bills got into the hundreds, but they both considered the big bills as the cost of Filer having steady work.

Besides the call from Filer, Abbey was looking forward to Labor Day. It would be a long weekend and Filer had promised to come back for her company picnic. She had been putting up with the produce manager's evil ways, and she knew once he saw she had a man, especially Filer, he would back off.

Now she would have to settle with Filer's call to hold her until he came back at the end of summer.

The telephone rang.

"Abbey darlin', how are you doin'," Filer started.

"Don't you darlin' me. We're way past darlin'," Abbey said, sounding as annoyed as she could.

"I'm just a working man, using the language of a working man. What's wrong with that?" Filer asked trying to sound hurt.

"Save it for the waitresses and barmaids Hon. There, how's that? I guess I know a little about working men," Abbey said. Then she continued, "Filer sweetie, you know Kylie and I are looking forward to seeing you on Labor Day. I promise to cook all of your favorite dishes and a special dish I've been saving up."

"Okay, you got me with the special dish. I'm looking forward to coming home. I guess I'm getting old and set in my ways. I'm just not the boomer I used to be. I'm even leaving the bars early, or not going at all. My crew got into a fight with bikers and I wasn't there to watch over them."

"You said your crew," Abbey said excitedly. "Did you get a promotion?"

"I did darlin'. I'm the foreman of a wire crew."

"Congratulations sweetie."

"My paycheck should go up a little. We can use the money can't we?"

Abbey could read between the lines and said, "I guess I'll have to raise your allowance a little. You can eat out once or twice a week and treat your crew to a couple of beers."

Filer felt bad momentarily for having tipped Glitter for a peak at her dragon's tail; then he recovered and said, "Maybe I'll treat Girlfriend to a fancy dinner."

"Girlfriend," Abbey said suspiciously.

"You know the stray cat," Filer said.

The two talked for a few minutes longer and then Filer told Abbey he had to get up early.

"You know, the new improved Filer Wilson; the kind of guy who goes to work sober, bright eyed and bushy-tailed."

"Okay lover. I'm really looking forward to Labor Day. I miss you," Abbey said.

"I love you and Kylie," Filer said, and got off of the phone.

Abbey hung up the phone and had a look at photo albums containing pictures of her, Kylie and Filer. She could put up with Stewart for another month until Filer came back to Albany.

Both Abbey's and Filer's last thoughts were that they would be going to bed alone.

CHAPTER 47

Rupert met Ozzie at the Broken Arrow. As soon as Ozzie sat down, Rupert started asking the same kinds of questions he'd asked Filer. After an hour of his questions Ozzie had had enough.

"Why are you interested in the Ontario job after all this time?" He asked Rupert. "Are you writing a book?"

"Well," Rupert said, "yeah I'm writing a book."

This stopped Ozzie, "What kind of book?" He finally asked.

"True crime," Rupert said. And then he admitted it might turn out to be only an article if he couldn't write enough for a book. "Right now it's looking good. If I put the murder and the line job together, it should be long enough."

Ozzie took a last drink of beer and stood up. "Well Rupert, I guess I should wish you good luck."

Rupert sat drinking alone for a few minutes and then left the Broken Arrow. Back at Filer's trailer he greeted Filer and then got out his duffle bag and started packing.

"I'm leaving now," Rupert said. "I need some privacy to finish my project. I'll probably end up back in Burley, Idaho to tie up a few loose ends."

Filer thought, "It's about time."

"Have a beer at the Bonanza for me," Filer said.

"Didn't you hear, they closed the Bonanza down a year ago," Rupert told Filer.

"Too bad, it wasn't a bad place to have a beer or two," Filer said.

Rupert finished his packing and he and Filer shook hands at the trailer door. Hesitating for a minute he got out his wallet and handed Filer fifty dollars.

"See you around 'Mad Dog'," Rupert said.

"Via con Dios amigo," Filer said.

Rupert looked at him in surprise and said, "Whatever."

CHAPTER 48

While the assembly and erection crews hustled to keep ahead of the wire crews, Filer with his crew and two other crews worked on preparing their thirteen tower stretch of the project for wire.

With materials on board Filer loaded the crew into the Highline flatbed truck. They were used to the postcard scenery they drove through every day, so most of the crew slept, grabbing an extra twenty or thirty minute nap. Once they arrived at the last tower to be rigged with travelers, Filer parked the flatbed. He took out binoculars and focused them down the line of towers stretching across the cleared mountain path.

At the farthest tower site he could see framed in the binoculars, an erection crew putting finishing touches on a tower. Another wire crew would arrive at that site and add travelers to the bells. After the wire crews finished with the travelers, the crews would be ready to start preparing sock lines to be strung using a helicopter.

Filer and Cowboy were on a tower, when the Wire Superintendent waved Filer down from the tower to his truck.

Filer noticed a young man wearing a big grin sitting on the passenger side of the pickup.

The Wire Superintendent looked up at the tower, "It's looking good. You've done a good job with this crew. I guess I picked the right man for the job."

Filer waited for the man to go on.

"Well Filer, you've also done a good job getting Jimmy on track. I would've made him a foreman earlier, but he needed to see how a crew runs the right way."

Filer thought, "Here comes the bad news," and then he heard Bradford say, "I'm taking Jimmy for foreman on the wire crew across the valley. He knows you, and he knows how you work. I hope you and Jimmy can continue working together to get the wire strung."

Filer raised an eyebrow at the Wire Superintendent. He now needed a new man to take Jimmy's place. Bradford correctly interpreted his raised eyebrow.

"I've got a new man here to replace Jimmy. This is Paul Moore. He's just come on with Highline, and he's had experience working wire."

Filer glanced across the pickup cab at the young man there. He didn't look old enough to be out of high school. It seemed like all of the new hands were young enough to be sons; sons of bitches more like it, came in Filer's mind.

"Here we go again," Filer came back to standing before the Wire Superintendent.

"How about telling Jimmy he's going to be a foreman," the Wire Superintendent told Filer. "You deserve a lot of credit for his promotion."

"Sure, I'll tell him."

Filer climbed the tower and stopped beside Jimmy. Jimmy looked at Filer, "Is everything okay?"

"Couldn't be better," Filer replied, and then added, "You better climb down and go with the Wire Superintendent."

"What?" Jimmy asked wide-eyed.

"Looks like some of the Filer good stuff rubbed off on you Cowboy. The Wire Superintendent wants you to be foreman on a wire crew."

Jimmy stared at Filer with amazement. Then he got a smile on his face as big as the kid sitting next to the Wire Superintendent.

"Don't get too happy Cowboy. Some guys are foreman for as long as it takes for the first screw-up."

When Jimmy lost the happy face, Filer loosened up. "You'll do okay. How about having a beer after work, one foreman to another?"

"You've got it 'Mad Dog'," then Jimmy beat Filer to the ground.

When Filer reached the ground the Wire Superintendent was driving off the site with Jimmy sitting beside him. Paul Moore had his gear in hand waiting for Filer to tell him what to do.

Filer introduced Paul to the other members of his crew.

"Paul is taking Cowboy's place. Tony, you and Greg are still on the ground. Okay, let's get busy; the travelers aren't going to hang themselves."

Once they were on the tower, Paul started talking and wouldn't shut up. "What do you think of the U.S. government?"

Filer had his mind on switching out a traveler and answered absent-mindedly, "Not much," when he actually meant to say, "Not very often." Filer's answer let loose a storm of words from Paul.

"The U.S. government is an illegal institution backed by Z.O.G., a Jewish organization created to take over world governments."

Filer, still concentrating on his work, barely heard what Paul had to say.

"Do you know there's a guy out in the woods not far from here living like a hermit? People say he doesn't have electricity or running water."

Filer heard, "….electricity or running water." The next speech Paul made also fell on deaf ears.

"The only legitimate form of government exists on the county level. The government in Washington D.C. collects taxes illegally and spends the money cooperating in an international kabala to rule the world."

Filer tightened the last bolt holding the frame for a bell and heard, "….rule the world."

"What's that?" He asked Paul.

"We should oppose all authority above the county, although, technically, even county officials who aren't members of the Posse Comitatus should be voted out of office and replaced by members of the Posse."

Now that Paul had his full attention, Filer said, "I try not to get mixed up in politics, so I guess I wouldn't be a good prospect for the Posse."

Paul shook his head, "That's just what makes you a good candidate for the Posse. Let me know if you decide to take a stand. The Posse needs men like you."

Now Filer had his eyes on Paul who had finished his work and was climbing down from the tower. He expected his time with Paul would be educational in a crazy kind of way.

Chapter 49

Ozzie called Filer with the news they now had money to get started on Shane's power line.

"Shane sent his G.C. a check for materials and labor for the first part of the project, "Ozzie explained. "Our material site will be on the property by his cabin. I figure we can rent an auger and buy the poles we need with this check."

"Sounds good to me," Filer agreed to Ozzie's plan.

Ozzie rented a back hoe with an auger attachment in Missoula and turned it over to Filer.

"We have sixty pole holes to dig. I figure it'll take us two weeks digging the holes after work," Filer consulted with Ozzie. "I'll have Rip-It-Up and Cowboy to help dig the holes. You make sure we have the beer," Filer kidded Ozzie.

Ozzie nodded his acknowledgment, "You have some nice country to work in out there."

"I see that country everyday. Just keep the cooler filled with beer."

After working the Highline job all day, Filer picked up Rip-It-Up and Cowboy and drove to Shane's cabin. Ozzie was already there with a cooler filled with ice and beer on his tailgate.

"Let's get this party started," Ozzie said.

Filer started up the back hoe with a chug and maneuvered it over the first hole to be augured. Rip-It-Up and Cowboy stood by as the auger bored into the mountain soil.

"You guys have to keep the dug up dirt away from the hole, "Filer yelled at Cowboy and Harold.

"I thought I hired on as a lineman," Cowboy complained.

"Put down the beers and start moving dirt," Filer insisted.

Harold moved close to the auger spiraling into the ground and scrapped at the mound of dirt. Cowboy put his beer down and followed Rip-It-Up.

"That's it then," Filer said, "Only fifty-nine more holes to go."

During the next week and a half, Filer, and his small crew, worked steadily, digging pole holes from Shane's cabin towards the county road and the local power line. Dave made periodic appearances keeping track of their progress and reporting to Shane.

CHAPTER 50

Abbey walked into the K&P Warehouse grocery store with a lot on her mind. She had accounts to balance and submit before the close of business. Most of the work was done and she didn't have anything serious to be concerned about. Still, deadlines meant concentrating on the books and things could come up to keep her from working on them-individual tills not balancing, cashiers not showing up; all of these were her responsibility. And she had to take her turn at the Customer Service window. All of these could keep her from finishing the last shift's cash receipts.

"Hey Abbey," Pat Fuller greeted Abbey.

"Pat," Abbey acknowledged her friend and then asked, "Did everyone show up?"

"We're lucky today. We have a full roster at least for the day shift."

"Great," Abbey replied and put her purse in the bottom drawer of her desk.

She got a cup of coffee, sat down and got comfortable before opening the folder with the previous day's receipts in it.

Using a calculator she started adding columns of figures and double checking the cashiers' totals. "I just need an hour of undisturbed time to finish up," she thought as she tapped in amounts from the individual sheets. Right at this moment the office door opened and stupid Stewart walked in.

"Good morning ladies," Stewart said.

Neither of the married women was inclined to be friendly. Stewart barely got a "morning" in response to his greeting.

This lack of response didn't seem to affect Stewart, and he leaned over Pat's shoulder to peak down her blouse. It was standard behavior for Stewart and both of the women expected this, and worse of him before he got his produce inventory sheets and thankfully left them in peace.

Stewart shuffled papers in the store's daily mail and picked up an inventory list of produce to be received. After glancing at the sheets he turned his attention to Abbey. He sat on a corner of Abbey's desk and said, "How long has your husband been gone?" He didn't wait for an answer and continued, "You know I'm always available for a dinner, just so you don't forget what it's like to go out on the town." The way Stewart emphasized 'out on the town' didn't leave much doubt what he was really talking about. Stewart winked at Pat. He'd given up on Pat, but wanted her to know he was still a player.

"Look Stewart, I'm busy now. Besides that, how many times do I have to tell you I'm not interested? How about getting your butt off of my desk and go catch some defenseless woman squeezing a peach?"

"Okay, but my offer still stands," Stewart replied, then added a comeback. "Just don't wait too long to come around girlie. You know tomatoes and peaches have a limited shelf life. You don't know what you're missing."

"I know what I'm missing and it definitely isn't you."

Abbey thought of threatening Stewart she was going to tell the store manager, and then decided she could handle Stewart on her own.

The man left the office with his inventory sheets. He also left both women hoping they'd seen the last of him for the day.

Pat said, "That man has the biggest ego I've seen and from what I've heard he doesn't have much of a reason for it, if you know what I mean," she laughed.

Abbey had never lacked for men in her life. Even after her divorce she had male friends she could count on to help her do repairs that needed a man's attention. The question she had to ask herself was why a man like Stewart who could see she was a married woman still insisted on bothering her.

And the fact she didn't want Stewart's attention really didn't have much to do with her being married. She just didn't like him, and no matter what he said would change her suspicions that all he wanted was the obvious. Once Stewart got what he wanted from a woman he would move on to the next conquest.

Her next door neighbors in Albany were married. Archie and Gloria were the same generation as her and Filer. When she told Gloria Filer would be working in Montana, Gloria volunteered, without any hesitation, her husband's help if she needed anything. Abbey knew Gloria meant it, and she also knew Archie would do his best to help her with whatever needed doing-in an emergency. That's the way Abbey saw it, as an offer to help out in an emergency only, and she kept their friendship on that basis. She didn't ask Archie to mow the lawn or do any of the chores Filer would normally do.

With Stewart out of the office Abbey quickly finished balancing the daily and then the monthly receipts.

Chapter 51

Gradually Filer calmed Paul down enough so that he could use Paul's energy, and put up with his verboseness and conspiracy theories.

Filer's crew worked one end of the Highline job.

Filer dropped men off at each tower, which they would climb waiting for a helicopter to fly over with a sock line.

On this day each of the crew members climbed individual towers. When the helicopter flew over they used catch ropes to corral the sock line. Each lineman threaded the sock line through the traveler on his tower. Once the sock line stretched from the first tower to the last tower it was attached at one end of the line of towers to a hard line. At this point the hard line would be attached to a board, a sort of Chinese handcuff that flexed so that it could loosen to be fitted over a wire and then pulled to tighten on the wire.

With the lineman on each tower, the wire would be pulled through the travelers by using a puller at one end of the line and a tensioner composed of six neoprene coated bull wheels at the other end of the wire.

As a teenager, growing up in farming country, Filer made money during the summer building fences for local farmers. In a very elementary way, building a power line was not unlike what he'd done back then.

Later, after he joined the Navy and ended up in the Sea Bees, because of his previous construction experience; he went to Vietnam. There he'd helped build military bases and air fields. At the end of his service he believed anything else he did after that wouldn't have the same scope and purpose. Now, the need of electrical power for homes and businesses supplied by Highline Electric and transmitted across the power line he was helping to build renewed his sense of accomplishing great goals.

This phase of line work was why Filer had become a line man. Being on the towers wasn't for everyone. An apprentice waited for a chance to go up the towers. After getting a chance, some apprentices decided climbing the steel towers wasn't for them. It took some a week or a month and some decided after one shift of working off a ladder with their body stretched between ladder and wires, tightening bolts that the job wasn't for them.

It definitely wasn't the easiest way to make a day's pay Filer decided after his first trip up a wooden pole, but it suited him. Now he decided he would become a steel climbing 'Mad Dog'. Somewhere in the back of his mind, if he had an instrument for looking into the future, it wouldn't be a telescope, letting him see a clear vision of the future. It would be more like a kaleidoscope, showing him jumbled fragments of work and family. For the moment he didn't need a master plan. He only needed to know he would be able to provide for his family and himself. True to his profession he was still a boomer at heart. It was the nature of his work.

Filer had helped build power lines through farmed flat lands and sagebrush covered deserts. He'd worked in Portland and Seattle doing distribution work. He'd done line work in all weathers. Probably the most difficult was working with the variety of supervisors and hands he'd been exposed to. He'd supervised crews and expected to continue being a supervisor. No matter if he didn't have a clear picture of where line work would take him; all he really knew was that when it stopped being fun he'd find something else to do. He'd been running heavy equipment when he started as an apprentice line man. There would always be something for him to do.

There used to be a time when Filer would have tried to explain some of this to an apprentice. Some had asked him what he thought of line work. Now he told them to give a good day's work for a good day's pay and let it go at that.

Whatever he said, the work and the bosses would have the final say in an apprentice's mind.

With the sock line reel at tower one and the wire truck at tower six, Filer, Paul, and three other line men were up towers ready to grab fly ropes and thread the sock line as the helicopter flew overhead.

Once the sock line and the hard line had been threaded through the travelers, Filer and the other linemen would guide the hard line and the wire through the travelers using the puller and tensioner so it could be sagged.

CHAPTER 52

Since Harold had divorced her, Leslie's new biker wannabe boyfriend Mortimer Nelson, known to fellow bikers as 'Boner Man' listened to Leslie's troubles in a Portland sports bar.

Mortimer 'Boner Man' Nelson wore a faded and frayed Levi jacket over a black T-shirt. The black T-shirt disappeared into black jeans over black work boots.

Mortimer was short sighted, but he refused to wear glasses so he squinted a lot. Mortimer made up for being short sighted by being mean as hell. He was just a touch of conscious short of being a sociopath. This quality is what attracted Leslie. She hoped she could persuade him to get her former husband's money.

From her perch on a bar stool, Leslie explained to Mortimer, "Harold said I was spending him into the poor house." Leslie frowned at her drink and then continued, "He set up his own checking account and put me on a budget. He said, "I'll give you my share of the household expenses but that'll be it. Then he divorced me." Leslie didn't explain that she had found ways around Harold's plan for keeping her on a budget and out of his pockets.

For a tough biker type Mortimer had an adoring look at Leslie that encouraged her to go on with her story.

"If Harold doesn't want to pay his alimony then I'll have to find another way to get the money he owes me."

Leslie had recently heard about Rip-It-Up's hold out stash from a mutual friend of the couple's before they had divorced.

Leslie put her hand on Mortimer's arm, "You can help me can't you, Mort?"

No one called 'Boner Man', Mort. While he was infatuated with Leslie and her well-groomed good looks, he was letting his status as a wannabe biker slide. Once his fascination with her ended he would reduce her to just another of his Old Ladies.

Leslie had to have seen the hard luck women who hung around the Get Lucky bar, but her judgment on this point was temporarily clouded. She had a plan to get her hands on Harold's hidden stash and it involved Mortimer. If and when this happened she didn't realize she could end up without any money; and being treated much worse by Mortimer.

'Boner Man' asked Leslie, "How much money does ole Rip-It-Up have stashed away?"

Leslie should have taken a clue from the greed oozing out of Mortimer's voice.

"A reliable source told me he has a money belt with thirty thousand dollars in it. Harold probably took it with him to Montana."

"Where, exactly, is Rip-It-Up now?"

"As far as I know he's still in Deer Lodge, Montana playing in a bar called the Broken Arrow."

"We'll have to make a little road trip to Deer Lodge," Mortimer said. He looked at Leslie like he expected her to make the trip with him.

"No," Leslie responded negatively to Mortimer, "I can't go. It would be too easy for the police to say I went there to get the money. No, I'll stay here until you get back, with the money."

Leslie's ability to trust a less than trust worthy man reflected the manner in which she had handled Harold's money when they were married. A woman with better sense wouldn't trust Mortimer 'Boner Man' Nelson within a mile of Harold's thirty thousand dollars.

"Have it your way," Mortimer said and tipped his glass to get the last drops of his drink.

CHAPTER 53

The Broken Arrow didn't have a band playing on Wednesdays, so at eight in the evening Harold stood on Filer's front door step and knocked on his door.

Inside, Filer heard Harold knocking, and standing up from his easy chair he lowered Girlfriend to the floor and went to answer the door.

"Hey there Rip-It-Up, come in," Filer invited Harold into his trailer.

Harold squirmed a little on the sofa making himself comfortable and said, "'Mad Dog', I need to ask a favor of you."

Filer asked Harold if he wanted a beer.

"No thanks Filer. I'd better concentrate on telling you what I've got to say."

"Sounds serious," Filer said, watching the concerned look on Harold's face.

"Well you know Leslie and I are divorced." Harold had explained his situation to the after hours crew building Shane McLane's power line. Harold stopped talking while he thought about what he wanted to say next. "Leslie hasn't taken it too well."

Filer waited patiently for Harold to go on. Girlfriend brushed against his legs with her tail up in the air.

"Now that we're divorced Leslie gets alimony, but she wants more. Anyway over the years I've put a little money away for an emergency fund-about thirty thousand dollars. It sounds like a lot," Harold said and smiled. "But in my day I made a hell of a lot more than that. Then when I married Leslie she started spending money faster than I could make it. And she kept spending it for the next ten years."

Filer lifted Girlfriend onto his lap and waited for Harold to go on.

"Since we've been divorced I heard Leslie has been hanging out at a biker bar in Portland where I did a couple of gigs. She thinks I don't know what's going on, but I have eyes and ears all over the place." Harold smiled a smart ass kind of smile when he said eyes and ears. He noticed Filer maintained a level expression, apparently not impressed, so he went on with his story.

"Leslie heard about my emergency fund because I got drunk and bragged about keeping the money. Now, from what I hear, she's after a biker wannabe she hooked up with to come after me and get the money for her. And, well I don't want to put the money in a bank where Leslie's lawyer can find it; so I have the money here with me in Deer Lodge."

"Wait a minute Harold. You're telling me you've got thirty thousand dollars on you right now."

"That's right Filer; the money is in this money belt." Harold pulled a money belt, with full pouches, out of a bag he'd brought with him. He held the money belt out to Filer and said, "Go ahead, take it." His voice held a surprising tone of command.

"If I do take it, what do you want me to do with it?"

Harold patted Girlfriend on the head when she left Filer and came to stand at his feet. "I have a feeling all of this will pass in a couple of weeks. If you can hold on to the money belt that long I believe I'll be in the clear. Leslie's new boy friend will lose patience with her and she'll have to find a new way of taking care of herself. Once that happens I'll find a new place to put my stash. Right now, I just have a hunch the money will be safer with you."

It occurred to Filer that holding Harold's money wouldn't be any safer for him than it would be for Harold. Still, it was hard for him to refuse Harold's request. "How long will it take before you'll feel safe enough to take the money back?"

"Three weeks should do it; definitely only one month. Then I'll put the money in a safe deposit box."

"I've got a suggestion," Filer said, "Why don't you just put it in a safe deposit box now?"

Harold developed a hurt expression, "You don't want to help me out?"

"I didn't say that Harold. But you know it might be safer in a bank than with me."

Girlfriend sat in the middle of the narrow living room floor looking wise. After a month of testing Filer, she had finally moved into his trailer with no reservations. It had been a good decision on her part because she had become the newest member of the Wilson household. Now Filer, to the best of his abilities, wouldn't let anything happen to the stray. It must have been this kind of commitment that Harold sensed in Filer.

"One month Harold; at the end of one month I'll be returning the money," Filer said as he accepted the money belt from Harold.

"Good," Harold said, It was obvious a weight had been lifted off of him.

Chapter 54

When Filer, Cowboy and Rip-It-Up finished digging the pole holes, Ozzie returned the backhoe to the heavy equipment rental place in Missoula and paid to rent a pole truck. At twenty poles per load Filer made three trips from Missoula to the material site behind Shane's cabin.

Ozzie used his crane to unload the poles. Later the poles would be transported to each site and set in the holes using Ozzie's crane.

Over the next week, after the day's work with Highline, Filer, Cowboy and Rip-It-Up worked with Ozzie to place and level poles before filling in the dirt they had removed with the auger. It had been three weeks since they started on the job.

CHAPTER 55

Just as Abbey hung up the phone Kylie walked in the door.

"Hi Sweetie, how was work?"

Kylie went to the fridge and poured herself a glass of orange juice.

"It was okay. We're having a sale on the kind of blouses you like. If you come in and pick one out I'll buy it with my discount."

"That's nice, I'll try to get in before the sale ends," Abbey said. "Filer called. He's still working on his extra job."

Kylie got a dark expression on her face, "He could come home on weekends."

Abbey explained, "You know he'd come home if he didn't have the extra job."

"I know mom. I just miss him."

"You know how it goes, the job in Montana will be done when the weather turns bad, and then we'll have Filer here underfoot. When he's here we'll all be wondering when he'll be going back to work."

"I know that too mom," Kylie admitted.

Abbey watched Kylie finish her juice and start to walk out of the kitchen. "What are you going to do now?"

"Gil and I are going to the mall to see a movie."

"What movie?"

"It's something with Shane McLane in it."

Abbey smiled and said, "That's the extra job Filer is doing. He's building a power line for Shane McLane."

"No way!" Kylie exclaimed.

"Yes way. I asked Filer to get you an autograph."

Kylie came back into the kitchen and hugged Abbey.

"Thanks mom."

"You're welcome, but let's wait and see if he gets the autograph. You know how shy your father is," Abbey said and laughed.

CHAPTER 56

Shane McLane sat at a front table in the Broken Arrow with Ferra, his girl friend, listening to Rip-It-Up on the stage.

"You really get off on this country rock stuff, don't you," Ferra kidded Shane.

"This is authentic, you know. Not some L.A. drug store cowboys. Look around at the crowd here. These are all Montana people."

"Okay, I get it. What I want to know is what makes these people any better than an L.A. crowd. I mean people are just people."

"Come on Ferra, you know better than that. In L.A. most of the crowd would have an agenda; not in the bar to listen to the music, maybe there to be seen or to see who is there."

"You don't think that kind of thing goes on here?"

"Could be, but definitely not on an L.A. level; most of the working men here are drinking a beer after work to relax so they can go home and sleep for five or six hours, then get up and go to work the next day."

Ferra said, "How many of these guys are Shane McLane fans? You know it takes a certain amount of sophistication to become a movie fan."

"What are you trying to say Ferra?"

"The so called real people here probably have real lives and don't use the movies as escapism. Where would our kind be without the L.A. crowd?"

"So you might have a point," Shane admitted. He sipped at his beer and smiled. "Can we just enjoy the music?"

Ferra smiled at Shane and let him off the hook.

Shane sat for a minute more listening to Rip-It-Up and the Misfits, and then said, "We better go. I have to get up early so I can climb some poles with the linemen building my power line."

Chapter 57

The weekend morning came too early for Filer. He could have slept until noon, but today he, Cowboy, Rip-It-Up and Ozzie were going to start framing the poles they'd set. As a bonus, the movie star, Shane McLane would be on site to help out. Filer could hardly wait. After a quick breakfast, during which Filer prepared food for himself and Girlfriend he told Girlfriend to guard the place until he got back, then he left the trailer park heading for Shane's power line.

On site, the other hands had arrived and they were waiting for Filer. Shane McLane waited with them in his old Ford pickup. "I've got to ask him why he drives that old beater," Filer thought.

While the rest of the crew sorted the material and tools they needed for the job, Filer took Shane to his pickup and motioned to the gear laid out there. There were two sets of gear, one for Filer and a set of old gear he used as a back up in case he left something at a site.

As he put each piece of his gear on he explained its function to Shane. "This is the tool belt. It carries wrenches, hammers and whatever else you need on the day. He watched as Shane followed his example and put on the tool belt. "This is a safety belt. We call it a scare strap," Filer showed Shane the long, wide, belt shaped leather strap. Along with your hooks, it's what keeps you on the pole." Filer draped the scare strap over his shoulder. Then he put on his hooks, tightening them securely to his high topped boots. Shane had slung his scare strap over his shoulder and tightened up his own hooks. Finally Filer handed Shane a pair of leather gloves and said, "The gloves protect your hands from splinters."

Shane laughed and said, "All we need now is a camera crew and a director yelling action."

Cowboy and Ozzie worked together while Filer coached Shane.

Following the traditional training method, Filer started Shane up a pole ahead of him. Once Shane had his scare strap around the pole and his hooks dug in off the ground, Filer mounted the opposite side of the pole slinging his scare strap under Shane's. Using this method, if Shane slipped, Filer could stop him from burning the pole by catching Shane's scare strap with his own.

Shane climbed halfway up the pole and had to stop and catch his breath.

"Take a deep breath and enjoy the scenery," Filer instructed Shane.

Shane breathed deep the pure mountain air and looked across the surrounding forest. He relaxed and then said, "So this is line work."

"This is a little part of it," Filer replied, "but you aren't carrying any tools or hardware."

"What do we do now?" Shane asked.

"We climb to the top of the pole and rig a line so Rip-It-Up can send us up the hardware we need to finish framing out the pole."

"Okay, let's do it," Shane said.

Shane McLane, action movie star, started climbing again. After advancing fifteen feet further upward he miss stepped and lost his grip on the pole. With his heart beating wildly, he started to burn the pole, until his scare strap caught on Filer's belt; and Filer reached out to grab his shoulder.

"Hold it there Pard; we've got a way to go before we start down again."

Shane righted his self and reset his spikes into the pole. Once he was situated, he started climbing until he was even with Filer.

"Thanks. I guess I would have been on the ground if you hadn't caught me."

"That's why my belt is under yours," Filer made his point. "You owe me a beer after work."

Once they reached the top of the pole Filer rigged a hand line so Rip-It-Up could send up hardware. He tossed the hand line to the ground and they watched it fall to where Rip-It-Up could get it and attach it to the hardware they needed and pull it up to them.

Filer attached the hardware and a bell to the pole, and told Shane, "The next pole is yours."

By the end of the day, under Filer's directions, Shane had learned how to climb and rig power poles. When both men were on the ground Shane invited Filer to have a beer with him after work.

"Come out to the cabin after you get cleaned up and I'll buy you a beer."

At his trailer, Filer got cleaned up. He was excited to be invited to Shane's cabin even if he didn't show it. He took time to pet and feed Girlfriend. While feeding the stray he asked her if she was impressed with movie stars. Girlfriend continued eating the cat food, and didn't have anything to say.

"Okay then, I'll take that as a no.

Hold down the fort Girlfriend, and I'll be back in a little while."

Driving the private road to Shane's cabin Filer estimated they had a little more than half the job done. If everything went well it would take another week and a half to finish the work. When he arrived in Shane's driveway he parked beside the ten year old Ford pickup Shane drove. He walked a short distance to the cabin door and knocked.

Shane answered the door, "Hi 'Mad Dog'. Thanks for coming."

Filer took the hand extended to him and shook it. He felt himself gently being pulled into the cabin.

Shane pulled two bottles of Coors out of a cooler and pried the tops off with an opener mounted on the side of the bar.

"So you didn't think much of my movie," Shane said with a smile.

Filer took a drink of the Coors and then answered, "I was probably so tired I couldn't keep my eyes open. Most days I work a ten hour day. And we're not talking sitting behind a desk. Get me in a place with little or no lighting and my body's first reaction is to catch a little nap."

"I understand," Shane sympathized, "the last thing I want to do after ten or twelve hours on the set is to go watch dailies. But if I want to have an idea of how I'm coming across, I have to make the effort," Shane finished by taking a sip of beer while raising his eyebrow.

Filer admitted, "Don't worry about keeping up with me. There's no way in hell I could be an actor, whether it's easy or not."

"How high are those steel towers you're working on now?" Shane inquired.

"The ones on this job are one hundred fifty to a hundred seventy-five feet tall."

"And you go to the top of them, don't you."

"Every once in a while," Filer said.

"Well, I'll admit I have a thing about heights," Shane said. "In my pictures that's when they bring in a stunt man."

Filer accepted Shane's explanation with a doubtful expression.

"I know it's hard to tell when the stunt man takes over," Shane said.

"If you worked on my crew I could get you over that in one week."

"Really, all it would take would be one week."

Filer laughed, "Yeah, one week would be all you'd get, and then you'd be a ground man for life."

Shane laughed along with Filer. "I could probably make a spear carrier out you."

"A spear carrier?"

"You know; one of the guys who comes on stage and stands in the back ground holding a spear."

"No thanks. I'll keep hiking poles for a living."

"I was just kidding 'Mad Dog'. If you ever decide you want to try another career, come to Hollywood and look me up. I'll get you on as a gaffer or a grip."

"I'll give it some thought," Filer said without admitting he didn't have a clue what a gaffer or a grip did. "Thanks for the beer," Filer said and stood up from the bar.

"Thanks for coming out," Shane thanked Filer and then explained. "I've got to get back to tinsel town, so I'll trust you and Ozzie to finish my power line. When I come out again we'll have a real party."

Chapter 58

Once Leslie knew about Harold's emergency fund she had to have his hold out stash. She knew he wasn't going to just hand it to her, so her plans for getting the money now involved Mortimer. If she had to be his 'Old Lady' until the deed was done, "Well, she'd been with worse before and after her marriage to Harold. He really had dragged her to the most awful places playing gigs with his band."

Leslie didn't hate Harold, she just liked money more. Sitting at the Get Lucky sports bar waiting for Mortimer to arrive; she went over her plan for getting the money from her ex husband. She drank a Cosmopolitan slowly and glanced at the door between sips. Getting near the end of the drink Mortimer 'Boner Man' Nelson launched himself into the bar.

'Boner Man' spotted Leslie and took the bar stool next to her. "Have you thought about what I said?" He wanted to know. The last time they were together, he had suggested Leslie should sell her house, give him the money and move into his trailer. Leslie considered the suggestion for two seconds before wondering if she'd really picked the right man to help her get Harold's hold out stash.

"I can't sell the house until the housing market is right," Leslie lied. "You don't want me to lose money do you?" Leslie asked Mortimer.

Mortimer ordered a straight shot of Tequila. When he looked Leslie in the eyes to answer her, she felt a tremor of fear go down her spine.

"You don't think I know what you're up to," Mortimer said. He tilted his head back and finished the shot. "One way or another I'll get my pay," he informed Leslie. He put one hand under her chin, pushed her head back and kissed her with the taste of Tequila still on his lips.

Leslie decided she would have to think faster if she was going to keep a step ahead of the 'Boner Man'.

Chapter 59

Abbey called Filer and wanted to make sure he would be back in Albany for the Labor Day weekend. She needed to be with him; an evening out with the girl's could only go so far.

"You're the woman Hon. You know, I'll be there for your company picnic. I can smell the barbeque already. And that's not all I'm looking forward to old girl. I hope you're ready to spend some quality time with 'Mad Dog', if you know what I mean."

"That depends on you old man. I have a short honey do list myself, if you know what I mean."

CHAPTER 60

Ozzie and Filer talked about how they would run the wire for the power line.

"There's no way I can ask Highline for equipment." Filer was adamant. "I don't want to do anything to ruin my chances of getting on as a regular hand."

"You're right," Ozzie agreed.

"But I might be able to make a call to an old friend of mine who runs a boomer outfit in Oregon. I think I could borrow as many travelers as we need."

"Sounds good to me," Ozzie approved. "So once you get the travelers up I'll get the wire on a flat bed truck and we'll get started."

It took Filer one phone call to get the travelers they needed lined up. Early on a Saturday morning Filer left his trailer to drive twelve hours to Oregon to fetch the travelers. It was too late the next day to do any work on the power line when he arrived back in Deer Lodge, so he called Ozzie and told him to pass the word they would have to wait until Monday evening to get started hanging travelers.

Filer was relaxing when he got a call that surprised him. "Glitter, what's up?"

"Filer, I need help."

"What's wrong?"

"The owner of Fred's is cutting back on expenses so I lost my job as a dancer."

Filer got it. "Well, I can loan you a little money, but I have a family."

"I didn't lose my cocktail waitress job, so I can get by. But I have a plan. I applied for a small business loan. I want to open a beauty salon. I thought I'd see if I could put together enough money to pay a down payment on the shop I found."

"Well, I don't have that kind of money girl. I could loan you enough money for groceries and a month's rent, but that's about it."

Glitter thanked Filer, "I knew you'd help out. Like I said, I can get by, and I'll probably find another job until I get my small business money."

Filer was ready to hang up when he remembered Rip-It-Up's money belt. Rip-It-Up had left it for him to take care of and he didn't feel comfortable keeping it in his trailer, so he told Glitter he might be able to help her if she could meet him at his trailer in Garrison.

CHAPTER 61

Leslie put pressure on 'Boner Man' to figure out a way to get Rip-It-Up's hold out money. "You can't get it sitting here," Leslie started in on Mortimer. She didn't know how she was putting herself in danger-first by nagging a bad ass wannabe biker, and second-she was misjudging her influence on Mortimer.

"You don't act like any Old Lady I've ever had. And I'm getting a little sick of hearing you whine about your ex's hold out money when you could make a lot of cash by selling that house of yours."

Leslie may have sensed the danger emanating from 'Boner Man', but she said, "I told you I'm not selling the house. We'll have plenty of money once we get Harold's hold out money." Leslie plunged ahead by saying, "If you haven't got a plan, I've got one."

Mortimer looked at the slight woman sitting beside him and wondered where all the anger was coming from. He understood his long standing grudges against the world in general, but he had a little harder time figuring out why Leslie couldn't let go of her ex's money.

"You know I'm going to get part of that money for my efforts," he informed Leslie.

Leslie didn't like the idea of Mortimer getting even a small part of Harold's stash. In her mind that meant getting the money away from one loser and turning it over to another loser. This was where her plan fell apart and she was thinking of a way to remedy the problem. Vaguely, this nebulous plan involved using Mortimer and then leaving him out in the cold. To her, this plan had a lot of merit. All she had to do would be to make sure she got the whole stash from Harold and then she could leave Mortimer in the dust. In the meantime she'd have to play Mortimer until she could maneuver him into getting the stash.

"It's simple," she started to explain her plan for getting Harold's money, "you grab Harold and you get him to turn over the cash. How you convince him to give you the money is up to you."

"It's simple if you're just thinking of grabbing a man. It isn't so simple if you're the one doing the grabbing."

"What do you mean? Harold doesn't have a body guard, and it will be easy enough to find out where he'll be when you grab him. He's performing at the Broken Arrow bar in Deer Lodge, Montana. It's a small town. How hard could it be to find him there?"

Mortimer explained, "It probably won't be hard to find Harold, but at the end of the day, grabbing a man is called kidnapping. And there is a felony charge for kidnapping."

Leslie got indignant against her better judgment and said, "For a share of thirty thousand dollars you have to accept some risks."

Despite their exchange up to this point, Mortimer was hoping to get lucky with Leslie before the evening was over, so he gave in to her and tried to make peace.

"I am going to take a risk. I just need to find the right crew to get the job done. You're sure Harold's got the money with him?"

"I'm sure he has a money belt with thirty thousand dollars in it. I got the information from a good friend of his."

"Okay," Mortimer said, "I'm going to get a couple of guys together, and we'll figure out how to snatch Harold."

As Mortimer explained his plan to grab Harold, it didn't sound like much of a plan to Leslie, but it sounded like progress over no plan at all and she let Mortimer back into her good graces for the time being. She let 'Boner Man' put his hands on her and nuzzle her on the neck in public. This was something she hated to do. Later, when Mortimer let the desire for sex fill his mind, she would get him to commit to a date for the abduction and robbery of her ex husband.

CHAPTER 62

Don Seifert rolled his dually into the show up area. He waited until Filer arrived and motioned him to his truck.

"Get in Filer; we need to talk."

Filer entered the passenger door and stepped up into Seifert's truck.

"I'm going to get right to the point. Are you going to stay with us after Labor Day?" Seifert offered Filer encouragement before he allowed him to answer the question. "You've done real well for a replacement hand, and I'd like to keep you on."

Filer had been hoping to hear from Seifert that he had a regular job with Highline, so he answered, "As far as I know Abbey won't say no to me having steady work, even if I have to live here for awhile."

Seifert responded, "I know how that goes. I've spent my share of time away from Mrs. Seifert. I don't think she ever liked it very much, but she knew we had to pay the bills, and she has always stuck with me."

There wasn't anything to say in reply, so Filer didn't say anything.

"Okay Filer, I'll talk to you again when you finish work on this section of the job."

Filer got his crew together and drove them to another mountain site. Each of them would be working a tower, threading the sock line and wire through travelers before the lines could be marked for sagging.

Across the deep valley, Cowboy and his crew were climbing towers to do the same work. By the end of the day they would be ready to clip wire.

CHAPTER 63

During the last week of work on Shane McLane's private power line Ozzie delivered the rolls of wire necessary to complete the project. On a Saturday morning Filer, Cowboy, and Rip-It-Up arrived at Shane's cabin. Ozzie invited the crew into Shane's kitchen for a cup of coffee and a short meeting.

"Fellers, we should finish up this job by the end of the week. Shane will be here by then and he wants to show off the cabin to his girlfriend," Ozzie paused for a minute. "This should be an easy week. All we have to do is reel out the sock line, attach it to the hard line; thread the hard line through the travelers and then pull the wire through.. After that we cornfield it and secure it to the insulators." Ozzie looked at the crew to see if they had any questions.

"We get the last pay check once we finish hanging the wire, don't we?" came from Cowboy.

"That we do," Ozzie confirmed. He waited for a minute again and drained the last of his coffee. "If that's it then let's get going. Filer, you and Cowboy hook the sock line to your pickup and Rip-It-Up and I will reel it out."

Filer and Cowboy hitched the sock line to the pickup's trailer hitch. Cowboy would sit in the back of the pickup and watch the sock line to make sure it didn't get fouled. Filer drove his pickup along the line of poles.

Ozzie paid the line out slowly. When the sock line ran out on the first reel Ozzie contacted Filer with a walkie and he stopped while Rip-It-Up spliced the sock line to another reel. With the sock line completely paid out the length of the power line Filer and Cowboy took turns climbing poles to hook the sock line into travelers. Once the sock line was threaded through the travelers the team started the hard line through the travelers.

Being careful to keep the wire off the ground the team pulled the hard line through the travelers until the wire stretched from one end of the line of power poles to the other end.

Finally with both ends of the wire dead ended; they all drove back to the cabin. Ozzie hoped the wire being dead ended overhead would prevent theft of the wire.

All that remained for the crew was to clip the wire to insulators along the three miles of private power line.

CHAPTER 64

Highline Electric gave its employees time off on Labor Day weekend. Filer told Ozzie he would be driving back to Albany, and that he couldn't work the extra job over the long weekend; and because of the distance he had to travel between Albany and Deer Lodge he'd asked Highline for an extra day off to visit his family.

"Abbey has been looking forward to this weekend and I've got to be there for her."

"That's fine 'Mad Dog'. I'm a married man too. Do what you've got to do."

Filer packed a bag and loaded it into his truck. He put Girlfriend into a pet carrier and told her, "You're going to make some new friends Girlfriend." Once he got to Albany he would see if Girlfriend could get along with the Wilson menagerie of pets. The Wilson family was very pet friendly and he hoped Girlfriend would be okay now that he'd adopted the stray.

After a twelve hour drive, Filer entered Albany looking forward to his homecoming. When he finally parked in his driveway he was glad he'd made the trip.

Abbey fed him his favorite meal and afterwards, with Kylie at work, they indulged in one of Filer's favorite past times. In the morning, when Abbey got ready for work, Filer watched her shower, towel off, and get dressed. The long trip home from Deer Lodge was worth it just for these moments. Before Abbey left she leaned over Filer in their bed and kissed him.

With Abbey at work Filer showered and relaxed. It felt great to nap in his bed. Girlfriend had been unsure about her place in the new surroundings with Bandit the cat, and Shay, a blue healer; but soon made herself at home, curling up to sleep at the foot of Filer's and Abbey's bed.

Eight hours later, when Abbey returned from work, she cooked Filer and Kylie another home cooked meal. Afterwards they watched T.V. together until it was time for bed.

The next morning, Filer came into the kitchen and saw Abbey preparing a picnic lunch for the company gathering. His first thought, after smiling at Abbey, was of the July 4th picnic he'd be missing in Riverview. He didn't know for sure, but Abbey's picnic probably wouldn't be as good as the Riverview picnics he'd attended with Clayton. He would miss getting drunk with Clayton and his uncle, and watching his mother give all of them a hard time for being drunk.

Abbey looked at Filer and read his mind, "I know it won't be the same as a Riverview 4th. Still," Abbey said, "we can go and be there long enough for me to say hi to my boss, then we can leave."

"I appreciate that," Filer said. After a minute Filer asked, "Where's Kylie?"

"She's staying with a girl friend. She'll be at the picnic this afternoon. She's really looking forward to seeing you Sweetie."

In Filer's eyes, Kylie had grown up fast. She had a job, a loser boyfriend, and now she wasn't at home so he could at least say hi.

"She's grown-up fast," Filer remarked to Abbey.

"She's sensible. She respects us. That's more than a lot of kids her age," Abbey replied.

Filer decided Abbey knew their daughter well enough to put his mind at ease. He had spent a large part of her growing up years away from both Abbey and Kylie. It was a part of family life Abbey took care of.

Abbey changed into a nice white blouse with lace cuffs and collar over a pair of new slacks. She twirled in front of Filer and asked his opinion.

"You'll be the best looking woman at the party," Filer said and kissed her.

"Alright," Abbey smiled. She grabbed the picnic basket and they left for the picnic.

It was a drive into Portland Filer had taken many times when he worked at the P.G. & E. Once they were in Portland, Abbey guided him to the city park where the company was having the picnic.

"Remember Sweetie, I want you to be on your best behavior. Really don't let that Filer charm of yours get us in trouble."

Filer smiled and said, "What do you mean about the Filer charm? I thought you liked that about me."

Abbey smiled and said, "I didn't mean getting in trouble with the women. I meant getting in trouble with me mister. I like the Filer charm just where I've got it."

CHAPTER 65

'Boner Man' drove to Deer Lodge over the Labor Day weekend. He wanted to see the man he would be kidnapping and extorting for thirty thousand dollars; the money that would soon be his money. 'Boner Man' didn't like Deer Lodge. His idea of a good time involved concrete and high rises. He liked sleazy strip joints and liquor stores on every street corner. Main Street towns didn't impress him. On the other hand he did like the Broken Arrow.

After checking into a motel, 'Boner Man' followed his nose for trouble directly to the Arrow. It was too early in the day for the band, so 'Boner Man' zeroed in on a female bartender and prepared to spend some time getting to know her.

Claudia Darnell never liked her name. Claudia came from her Grandmother. Claudia preferred Candy.

'Boner Man' sat at the U-shaped bar and watched Candy work. It didn't escape Candy that she was being watched. It wasn't the first time. Lonely guys came in all the time hoping to get lucky. Most of them were obnoxious, but harmless. Something about this guy, who had the nerve to introduce himself as 'Boner Man' made the hairs on the back of her neck stand up.

Mortimer ordered another draft beer, his third in three hours. He didn't plan on getting drunk-this was a reconnaissance mission.

"How about it Candy, just you and me after you get off work?"

"No thanks Mr. Boner," Candy said with as much sarcasm as she could put in her voice.

"Your loss," Mortimer said and watched as Rip-It-Up finally came on stage with the Misfits.

"So here he is," Mortimer thought. "Working him over might just be fun," he observed as the long-haired, rangy, lead singer rehearsed with his band.

Rip-It-Up had no idea his fate was being decided by the leather jacketed man at the bar.

CHAPTER 66

"What's wrong?" Abbey asked Filer.

"What?"

"You're frowning," Abbey explained.

"Just thinking of the Riverview 4th, I guess," Filer said.

"I know you miss Clayton," Abbey leaned closer to say, "We won't stay long, just long enough to eat some potato salad, some barbeque, and drink a beer."

Gathered around three picnic tables the K&P employees waved and yelled at Abbey. They motioned her to the company picnic.

Abbey waved back, and joined the party with Filer.

Including family members there were about thirty people at the picnic. They were all doing what people do at picnics. The more athletically fit had a soft ball game going. Men with beers in one hand and horseshoes in the other were gathered around horseshoe pits. Mothers watched their young children and gossiped with other mothers. Single men were seated at a table drinking until they had enough nerve to make passes at the single women. Abbey and Filer joined Pat Fuller and her husband Al.

Filer knew Pat from previous visits to the K&P, but he didn't know her husband.

Pat introduced the overweight object of her affection to Filer. "Filer, this is my husband, Al. Al is a third grade teacher," she declared proudly.

Al held his hand out over the table and Filer shook it.

"What do you do Filer?"

"I work steel towers," Filer answered.

"Skyscrapers?" Al asked for clarification.

"Depends on what you mean," Filer said.

"Well, I mean tall buildings," Al explained, not catching onto Filer's game.

Filer smiled at Abbey and then at Al. "I'm a lineman. I build power lines. Working out in the middle of nowhere in Montana, right now," Filer added.

"That's very interesting," Al replied, and looked at Pat. Pat nodded at him as if to say, "Okay honey, you've done your duty."

Filer sipped at a beer, watching the softballers taking pitches, getting hits, and running the bases. It was a fine day for a friendly softball game.

As she promised, Abbey said hi to her manager and the assistant manager. They both knew Filer and smiled his way after talking to Abbey. Both men made it a point not to get into lengthy conversations with the bearded man; this suited Filer. He knew their kind-all business with not much else to say.

The picnic table filled up with paper plates of picnic barbeque, favorite dishes brought from home, and empty pop and beer bottles. Filer was in the middle of telling Al a lineman's story he'd told enough times that it could only get better after a six pack of beer.

"He talked a lot on the way up the pole," Filer said, "but when he burned that pole he didn't have time to say much on the way down."

Al's eyes were fastened on Filer like he'd seen his third grader's eyes fastened on him after a particularly successful lecture. "Was the man hurt?" Al asked.

Just as Al asked his question a large man approached their table. He was wobbling a little.

"Whoa their partner, you shouldn't sneak up on a man like that," Filer said, giving him a friendly warning grin.

"Oh no," Abbey thought when she saw Filer facing Stewart, the lecherous, overbearing produce manager.

"Well, cowboy, if I wanted your advice I'd ask for it. I'm here to pay respects to Abbey," Stewart proclaimed, going into his full strutting rooster mode.

Filer gave Abbey a puzzled look.

Abbey gave Stewart a disgusted stare and shrugged her shoulders at Filer. "This is Stewart, Filer I think I mentioned him to you." Abbey returned to staring at Stewart and said, "He gets himself confused with a real man," Abbey said glaring at Stewart.

Stewart used poor judgment of his situation to make matters worse. "If I was married to pretty Abbey I wouldn't be working in another state and leaving her all alone," Stewart mumbled.

Filer looked at Abbey.

Abbey shook her head. She knew where this was headed if Stewart didn't shut up.

Stewart stumbled and put his hand on Filer's shoulder. Filer grabbed the produce manager's soft hand in a hand that was muscled from fifteen years of line work. Stewart winced as his fingers were squeezed together.

"I think you're at the wrong table, Stewart. If you back off now I won't have to kill you." Filer hadn't let go of Stewart's hand and continued to put pressure on it.

Stewart blinked and tried to pull his hand out of Filer's grip. Filer tightened his hold. Stewart put his full and considerable weight into breaking Filer's hold; and when Filer judged he was off balance enough, he let go and watched the big drunken man fall backwards, trying to regain his balance until he caught one foot behind the other and ended up taking a hard fall on his butt.

Al's expression said he didn't know whether to be shocked or to laugh at the produce manager's misfortune. He turned to Pat to gauge what his reaction should be. Pat had a hand to her mouth, covering a broad smile.

Pat removed her hand and smiled at Abbey. Abbey hoped Stewart was smart enough to get up and leave without making things worse. Both women knew Stewart had gotten exactly what he deserved.

Stewart wasn't the produce manager because of a total lack of brains, and he made the right decision after he crawled onto his knees and lifted himself off the ground. He gave Filer the mandatory death stare, but used what dignity he had left to walk away from the table.

Usually the disagreements Filer got into took a little more tussling to settle. This one brought a smile to his lips, and he winked at Abbey.

Dennis Perry

Abbey had to smile back at her husband. She knew Stewart had just escaped a beating from the 'Mad Dog' in Filer.

When Abbey had started gathering serving bowls into the picnic basket Kylie came to the table, hand and hand with Gil. "Dad this is Gil," Kylie introduced her boyfriend.

CHAPTER 67

Mortimer sat nursing his fifth draft beer. He'd turned his attention from Candy to Janelle. Mortimer recognized a working woman when he saw one, and so far Janelle looked like a good bet for a little action after the bar closed.

On stage, Rip-It-Up had given the crowd his version of *Lineman for the County*. Several boos went up from the locals, who were tired of the line crews hitting on their women.

'Boner Man' had scouted the Broken Arrow inside and out. He knew all the exits Rip-It-Up could use to leave the bar once it closed. When the time came he had a general plan in mind for grabbing Harold. For the time being 'Boner Man' closed the deal with Janelle. He didn't mind paying a buck or two for a good time, and if he got lucky, maybe their date wouldn't cost him anything.

As 'Boner Man' escorted Janelle out of the Broken Arrow, Rip-It-Up's girlfriend, Cherie, back in Deer Lodge from Saskatchewan, passed him at the front door. She gave the big man the once over. She wasn't impressed.

Cherie wore a leather jacket and tight leather pants. Two members of her girl gang followed her to an empty table in front of the performers' stage. Cherie had an attitude, and she didn't mind showing it. Pulling out a chair at the table, she sat down with her arms folded on the back of the chair.

Rip-It-Up spotted Cherie and dipped his guitar in her direction, giving her a big smile. Cherie made a small return salute to Rip-It-Up when he left the stage with his band members. After stowing their instruments in a small dressing room, Rip-It-Up and the band members returned to the bar area to join Cherie and her pals at their table.

"Hey lover," Cherie greeted Harold.

"Hey yourself," Harold replied.

Rip-It-Up, Taylor and Vaughn and the girls in Cherie's gang started getting to know each other. At last call Rip-It-Up suggested they should all go up to Shane McLane's place. He promised to show them around the cabin.

They all poured into Harold's Cadillac and thirty minutes later they were at the mountain cabin.

Harold remembered where Shane's G.C. hung his emergency key and went to the generator room to start the generator and get the key. He had a moment's hesitation before opening the front door, and then he felt Cherie crowding close to him. He felt the heat between them building. He turned the key and the small group crowded into the cabin entrance landing.

"My God," Cherie said, "McLane calls this a cabin."

"That he does," Rip-It-Up confirmed. "This is just a get-away place for when he wants to get away from Hollywood."

Taylor, the bass guitarist, brushed past Rip-It-Up and went straight to the bar. "Looky here babe, we've got booze," he yelled across the large open cabin first floor to Tawyna.

Rip-It-Up couldn't stop the party that followed. The best he could do, was try to control it.

When they had drunk the last shot of Tequila, and snorted the last line of cocaine, they found couches and beds that they fell into together. It had been a hell of a party.

Toward noon the next day the bedraggled group left a mess Rip-It-Up vowed to come back and clean-up.

CHAPTER 68

Kylie held her breath as Filer sized up Gil.

"You're too late for the barbeque," Filer advised the scraggly young male.

"Not a problem, man," Gil replied as if forgiving a fault on Filer's part.

Filer caught the tone in Gil's voice and mentally noted Gil's attitude.

Kylie held Gil's hand in a protective manner. In reality, she needed to see if Filer accepted Gil. So far she could tell Filer wasn't too impressed.

Gil spotted a cardboard six pack with a single bottle of beer left in the pack. He reached for the beer and Filer warned him, "I wouldn't touch that beer unless you brought a six on you I can't see."

Gil's hand stopped in mid air, and he looked at Kylie to be sure of what he'd just heard.

"Don't look at her. You got here late. That was your first mistake. Grabbing for that beer was your second mistake. Do you want to go for strike number three?"

The grungily dressed young man assumed a sour expression and looked again at Kylie for help. She didn't say anything.

"I'm out of here," Gil growled and dropped Kylie's hand.

Kylie stopped Gil by putting her hand on his arm and said, "Dad, can we just sit down for a minute?"

The 'Mad Dog' came out in Filer. "Gil wants to sit at the grown-up's table and he's not ready yet. He's not ready to take care of you. I think Gil wants you to take care of him. If he was on my crew he'd be a ground man for life; and probably not a good one at that."

"Thanks Dad," Kylie said with as much disdain as she could muster, and turned away from the picnic table to follow Gil out of the park.

Abbey, Pat and Al watched the two young people walk away and then they all looked at Filer.

Meeting their stares Filer grabbed the last beer and popped it open.

Nobody said anything for a minute until Abbey said, "You're right about Gil. He's not good boy friend material. He borrows money from Kylie and stands her up to go drinking with his friends."

Pat and Al sat silently, not wanting to get involved.

CHAPTER 69

Light filled the bedroom waking Filer up. Abbey snored softly beside him and he knew he was in Albany. Today he could have breakfast at home, and then he'd have to start back to Deer Lodge. He got out of bed to take a shower. Abbey needed her days off just as much as he needed his days off. He would let her sleep while he showered and got himself a cup of coffee.

The coffee maker burbled and Filer poured himself a cup. He was taking a drink when Kylie came into the kitchen. Kylie had changed from an adoring adolescent to a disdainful teen, almost overnight. It didn't do Filer much good knowing Kylie was a teenager and he should expect a change in their relationship. He didn't let it show, but he was disappointed when they didn't get along.

"Morning Dad," Kylie greeted him.

"Morning," Filer replied.

"Dad, I'm sorry about yesterday with Gil; but you're wrong about him."

"I hope so," Filer said. Abbey had explained they shouldn't forbid Kylie from going out with Gil. Forbidding her would only make matters worse. "That boy should learn some manners. If he comes around here on a regular basis, I'll figure it's my job to school him up a little," Filer warned Kylie.

"Why do you always think you know everything?"

"It's my job to know everything," Filer said smiling.

"I'm pretty sure you don't know everything," Kylie argued, standing up to the man who helped raise her.

Filer couldn't help himself, "Well there's a whole world out there just waiting to hear what you know."

Kylie poured herself a cup of coffee and walked out of the kitchen.

Filer had gotten the last word, but it didn't feel like he'd won the argument.

Abbey entered the kitchen with her hair wrapped in a white towel.

"I just saw Kylie go into her bedroom. Did you two make up?"

"Afraid not, but I think she left feeling a lot smarter than the old 'Mad Dog'."

"Why is that?"

"I couldn't convince her she should give up that loser Gil."

"That's too bad. I don't like Gil that much," Abbey said and poured a cup of coffee. She added a teaspoon of sugar and took a sip. "But she could have picked a drug dealing, smart ass instead of a plain loser."

"I can hardly wait to get back to Deer Lodge," Filer joked.

Filer picked up a piece of paper setting beside his cup of coffee and held it out to Abbey. "Here's Shane McLane's autograph signed for Kylie. I didn't get a chance to give it to her before she left."

Abbey accepted the autograph with a smile.

Filer had his pickup loaded and ready for the trip back to Deer Lodge. It was time to find Girlfriend and say goodbye. Filer thought the stray would be better off staying behind in Albany. After looking for her for five minutes he told Abbey he couldn't find her.

"I just want to make sure she is alright," he explained

"Where did you look?"

"I looked in the house and the yard."

"Well honey, I'm sure she'll turn up. We'll take good care of her. She's a member of the family now."

"Your right," Filer kissed Abbey. "I'd better go."

Abbey followed Filer out of the kitchen to his pickup. They were standing by the pickup, with the door open, when Girlfriend dashed around the corner of the house, jumped between Filer and Abbey and landed on the pickup seat.

"Looks like your lost stray is back," Abbey smiled and reached into the cab to pet the cat. When her hand got inches from Girlfriend, the stray bristled and hissed at her.

Filer couldn't help laughing.

"Go ahead and laugh. Your little friend is going back to Deer Lodge with you until she learns some manners."

CHAPTER 70

Ozzie inspected the McLane power line with Trina driving his truck. One half of the line was completed. Once the rest of the crew came back after the Labor Day weekend they could finish the work in a week and a half. The final payment would be a nice end of summer bonus.

At the end of the private lane, Trina parked the pickup. She and Ozzie wanted to take a quick look inside the cabin. Ozzie found the spare key in the generator room and the couple entered the cabin's front door.

"Oh my God," Ozzie said when they saw the mess left by Rip-It-Up and his friends. He saw overflowing ashtrays, empty beer bottles and glasses-some with lip stick prints, and furniture out of place with cushions scattered.

"It looks like a tornado hit this place," Trina exclaimed.

"I didn't know Shane was back in Deer Lodge," Ozzie remarked.

Trina started tidying up, "What if it wasn't Shane? What if it was someone on your crew? Didn't he say you could use the cabin while you were working out here?"

"He was just being a gentleman. He told us we could use the toilet instead of crapping in the woods. I'm sure he didn't mean drinking his booze and making a general mess of the place."

Trina looked around again and asked, "What do you want to do?"

"I'm not replacing the booze, but it wouldn't take ten or fifteen minutes to clean this mess up."

The two got busy and in a short time they had the cabin back in shape. Ozzie and Trina sat down and while they relaxed the sound of a vehicle stopping came to them from outside the cabin. Ozzie gave Trina a questioning glance. She shrugged her shoulders. Seconds later Rip-It-Up came into the living room.

"What are you doing here?" Ozzie asked Rip-It-Up.

"I guess you saw the mess we left last night. I fucked up Ozzie. I brought some friends out just to show them around the place and one thing led to another. Things got a little out of hand. I thought it would be best to get everyone out of the cabin; then I'd come back later and clean up the place. Looks like you guys beat me to it. Sorry about that."

"Shane didn't mean we could come out here and trash the place. He just offered us the use of the toilet."

"I know Ozzie. I fucked up. It won't happen again."

"You bet it won't. From now on, if you have to go, use the woods."

CHAPTER 71

The Tuesday after the Labor Day weekend Filer was back at work with his Highline Electric crew. It might not be fair that he'd left Abbey and Kylie to live more or less without him, but it was the only way he knew to make a living. Whatever happened between Abbey and Stewart and Kylie and Gil would play out without him. Here in Deer Lodge he had to concentrate on doing line work, which was what he knew.

"Okay, here's the materials list for today," Filer turned the list he'd scribbled over to Greg. "Get the gear into the truck and let's go to work."

Filer loaded Paul, Tony and Greg into the company truck and drove them to the mountain sites where the wire would be sagged.

At the far end of the valley, Cowboy ran a cat, tensioning the wire. Getting the wire sagged, involved using sighting guns to adjust the level of the wire between the towers. A lineman on each tower marked the wire so it could be clipped to bells.

Even though the right of way had been cleared up to two hundred feet surrounding the tower sites, Filer noticed the wire had become tangled in a lone snag on the valley floor. There was no tower near it, but it was in the path of the wire now being tightened across the valley.

"Hey Cowboy, you guys had better let off on the wire so I can clear it from a snag in the valley," Filer tried to communicate to the mountain site opposite his own tower.

"Say again," Cowboy said.

"The wire is hung up on a lone snag in the valley," Filer explained. "Can you clear it?"

"I can clear it if you let off on the wire," Filer yelled into the company phone.

"What?" Cowboy yelled back.

"Look out Buddy. Forget about letting off on the wire; that tree just snapped off and launched like a rocket. It'll probably come down somewhere between you and Deer Lodge."

"What?" Cowboy repeated.

"Forget about the snag," Filer spoke calmly into the radio.

At the end of the day Filer had a great story to tell at the Broken Arrow. He met Ozzie, Rip-It-Up and Cowboy at the Arrow before they left for the Shane McLane job.

"You should have seen that snag take off," Filer laughed when he told them about the lone tree in the valley that got launched like an arrow from a bow.

"Yeah, shit happens," Ozzie said, "Gents drain your glasses, we have a power line to finish," Ozzie put an end to the brief after work drinking session.

CHAPTER 72

On the private job, all of the poles had been framed and set, and the wire was dead ended on either end of the power line. All that was left to do was to clip the wire to the insulators.

With the wire hung from the borrowed travelers, Ozzie and Harold and Filer and Cowboy worked alternating poles attaching the wire to the glass insulators. The crew had leveled the wire by an informal method called corn fielding, a process of leveling by eyeballing the wire against the horizon.

With the wire attached to the last insulator the crew's job was done.

"There we are boys. It's a job well done. I'll let Dave know the connections are made and the power company can turn on the power to Shane's cabin," Ozzie patted Filer on the shoulder. "I think we've earned our bonus and the last payment. Right now I've got to get home and make sure Trina doesn't spend all the money I'm going to get paid. Filer, you take the crew to the Broken Arrow and put whatever you need on my tab. I already told Nancy you'd be coming."

Rip-It-Up said, "Looks like it'll only be you and Cowboy. I'm playing tonight."

"We'll send you up a beer or two, and as long as it's on Ozzie we'll buy the band a drink or two."

CHAPTER 73

At the Get Lucky sports bar in Portland, Leslie sat with Mortimer Nelson, a.k.a. 'Boner Man'. Leslie got on Mortimer's nerves by continuing to question him on when he would get her money from Harold.

"He'll get away with my money if you don't do something," Leslie insisted.

"I'm working on it," was all Mortimer would say.

"You've got to do better than work on it," Leslie demanded.

"You could help out by selling your house for operating cash," Mortimer countered her demand. "You know the trip to Deer Lodge and hiring a crew isn't free."

"I told you I'm not selling my house in this market."

"Well, that means me and my boys get a bigger cut of the money we take off of your old man," Mortimer said, testing Leslie's acceptance of his new plan.

"We'll see," Leslie said, turning to face away from 'Boner Man'.

'Boner Man' relented and laid out his plan of taking members of his gang to Deer Lodge so they could grab Rip-It-Up. He didn't go into details of what they would do to him to make him give up the thirty thousand dollars.

Later, after Mortimer got rid of Leslie, he gathered his crew in a corner booth and laid out his plan for grabbing Rip-It-Up. Both of the men were solid Aryans with spider webs, swastikas and various mythical animal tats. Stokes and Randy were 'Boner Man's' crones and were now in on his plot to kidnap Rip-It-Up Roberts.

"This isn't going to take long. I think Roberts will hand over the money before we have to break any bones."

"That's too bad. Breaking bones is my specialty," Randy bragged.

"Bull shit," Stokes said, "when was the last time you broke a bone."

Stokes winked at Mortimer. They both knew what was coming.

"What make you think I've never broken a bone?" Randy said.

"You're a pussy Randy. The worst you've done is pinched some broad's tit a little too hard."

"Okay you two, just be ready to go in the morning. Be at my place at ten o'clock. And we're not going on a picnic so both of you bring a piece."

'Hey Randy," Stokes kidded, "don't forget a hammer so you can break a bone."

"Up yours," Randy said.

Chapter 74

Filer, Ozzie and Trina were having margaritas at Ozzie's place. They were celebrating final payment on the Shane McLane job.

The local power company had tied in the power line to a hook up at Shane's cabin two days earlier.

"Believe it or not Shane invited us all to spend a weekend at his place in Hollywood anytime we want," Ozzie explained.

"What about you Filer? Are you planning to make a special trip to Hollywood to take McLane up on his offer?" Ozzie asked.

"Yeah right, I didn't lose anything in Hollywood. No need to go looking for something that isn't there in the first place."

Trina said, "Well personally, I wouldn't mind spending a little time in tinsel town. You know; dinner with the stars, and all that; get an autograph or two." Trina gave Ozzie an inquiring glance to see if he was interested.

"I agree with Filer. Nothing there for me, but if you want to go see Mr. Shane McLane on his home turf I'll take you."

Trina smiled at Ozzie clinking his drink with hers. "Is anyone ready for another drink?" She asked.

"Not me." Filer said, "I've got to get to the trailer and let Girlfriend out. She'll be pissy if I don't.

CHAPTER 75

It was after midnight and Detective Lance Crowder and his partner Detective Wayne Porter were tracking a Seattle crew that high jacked freight trucks; drove them to a deserted warehouse, unloaded the merchandise and stored it there until they could get it fenced. Once the freight trucks were unloaded, the crew drove them to another part of the city and abandoned them. The crew had operated successfully for several months. Now detectives Crowder and Porter were close to catching them red-handed with the stolen merchandise.

Leaving their unmarked police car, the detectives drew their service revolvers. They proceeded along the perimeter of the warehouse.

"What do you think Lance, are you sure Dexter and his crew are here?"

"You heard Marvin the Mouth tell us where we could find them. Anyway, do you have someplace else to be?"

"I'm with you Lance. Do you think we should call for back up?"

"No way; what happens if Marvin did yank our chain? We call for back up and they get here and there's nothing here, and we look like rookies. We wait until we find them, then we'll call for back up."

"Okay Lance. That's why you're calling the plays man."

"Remember college, you saved my butt on the football field. You were a hell of a guard. I couldn't have asked for better."

Now the two detectives heard a freight truck pulling up to the warehouse entrance. When the truck stopped and a man got out and opened the warehouse door, Lance said, "Okay, let them get inside the warehouse, then we'll call for back up."

Dexter, the gang leader, drove the freight truck through the open door and into the warehouse.

Once the truck was inside, Detective Porter called for back up. He told Lance that back up was on the way.

Inside the warehouse, Dexter had his men start unloading stolen televisions and stereos from the high jacked truck.

"What do we do now?" Wayne asked Lance.

"You know patience is a virtue," Lance replied.

"Now we wait for back up to arrive, unless something goes wrong."

"I'm right behind you boss."

"That's very comforting," Lance said.

The two men waited for back up to arrive. But after a few minutes impatience got the better of Lance. Wayne could tell Lance was getting tense.

Finally Lance broke his nervous silence, "First we look inside and see what's happening."

The two men edged carefully up to the open warehouse door and peered inside. They saw the piles of stolen televisions and stereos the crew had unloaded from the freight truck. Lance watched inside for a minute longer and spotted Dexter. He pulled back from the doorway and said to Wayne, "You know the smart thing to do would be to wait for back up."

"I don't follow you," Wayne said.

Lance whispered, "This is our chance for a major bust."

"What do you mean?"

"I'm thinking we should go in and make the arrest. You know, the Butch and Sundance thing when they go out the door with guns blazing."

Wayne replied, "Er….Lance, Butch and Sundance were the bad guys and they got mowed down by the Mexican Federales."

"Cut, excellent work gentlemen. We'll break for lunch now. Everyone is back here in one hour." Director Lawrence Latimore set his bull horn down and got up from his director's chair.

Shane McLane started walking off the set when Lawrence called after him, "Shane, my man, wait up a minute," and hurried to walk beside his star. "What are you doing when we wrap? I may need to get in touch."

"I'm going to Montana. I've got a cabin there."

CHAPTER 76

A fire warning sign on the edge of the National Forest pointed to Extreme Fire Danger.

From the top of a Highline tower Cowboy could see the forest surrounding Shane McLane's cabin. Not far from Shane's cabin at a camp ground shaded by pine trees, the Reyes family from New York packed their camping gear for the return trip to New York City. Jorge Reyes kissed his wife and hurried his children, "Samantha, Jorge Jr., come on guys it's time to get on the road."

Jorge Jr. followed his older sister into the back seat of the Chevy Suburban. With the family aboard, Jorge Sr. shifted the Suburban into gear and left the camping place behind. Unfortunately the family station wagon kicked a spark into the dry grass around the camp ground leaving an orange glow gaining strength on the forest floor.

Left to burn, the spark expanded into a brush fire and expanded upward into the lower branches of the pine trees. By the time a forest service watch station reported smoke, the fire covered several acres.

Cowboy called Filer on the company radio. "Filer this is Cowboy."

On the ground, at a nearby tower, Tony waved at Filer, "Hey Filer, Cowboy's on the radio. He wants to talk to you."

Filer climbed down a leg of the tower and took the phone from Tony. "This is 'Mad Dog'. What's up?"

"'Mad Dog', did you see the smoke over by Shane's cabin?"

Filer looked around the site but couldn't see smoke from the ground level. "I don't see any smoke," Filer came back on the phone.

"Well go back up top and look," Cowboy insisted.

Filer replaced the radio receiver in its cradle, and climbed back up the tower until he could oversee the surrounding forest.

"Holy shit," Filer exclaimed when he spotted the plume of smoke hovering over the forest by the power line they had just completed. Filer hustled back down the tower leg and grabbed the phone. He called Cowboy and let him know he'd seen the smoke. Then he called Ozzie and told him about the fire. "You better call Dave," Filer suggested.

"Okay, I'll call him. We'll see what Shane wants to do."

Twenty minutes later Lawrence Latimore called cut.

Shane listened to Dave on the telephone in his on set trailer. "Hire a couple of guys to help you keep an eye on the cabin and the power line. Do what you can to keep them from burning, but stay safe."

Dave called Scott Barrow his foreman and told him to be ready to go to Shane's cabin; then he jumped into his pickup and headed for Scott's home. Five minutes on route seemed like an hour until he pulled into Scott's driveway. Scott scrambled into the truck. Twenty minutes later the two men arrived at Shane's cabin where they could see the column of smoke rising in the forest.

Filer watched the fire burning as he worked on a tower clipping wire. The fire claimed part of his attention so that he violated Ozzie's advice from long ago. He wasn't keeping his mind on his work. The wire he was transferring from a traveler to a bell slipped out of place and twanged against the metal tower. He'd been lucky he wasn't injured. Forty five minutes of work wasted because his attention had drifted. Filer had been doing the job long enough that the minute of unexpected action hadn't scared him, it only surprised him. He rigged a winch to bring the wire back into position for clipping it to the bell. Throwing a nylon winch strap under the loose wire; Filer caught the winch strap, bringing it over the wire, where he threaded it back into the winch. With the winch strap in place he winched the wire back into position so he could clip it to the bell.

At the end of a long day, Filer and Cowboy returned to the Garrison show-up area. Both men hurried into Filer's pickup and he drove them to Shane's cabin. Smoke drifted heavily over the lane to the cabin. But the fire hadn't touched either the power line or the cabin. In the cabin driveway Filer stopped the pickup and found Dave and Scott standing by with fire fighting tools in the back of Dave's truck.

"We're not through here yet," Dave uncoiled a regular garden hose from the back of the truck and carried one end to the cabin and screwed it to an outlet.

"We've seen some sparks floating overhead. I'm going to wet down the cabin, especially the roof." When Dave tried wetting down the roof he couldn't reach it from the ground. He looked around for a ladder and couldn't find one. Filer watched Dave trying to wet down the roof from the ground and said, "Let me have the hose." Dave gave Filer the hose and stood back to watch what Filer would do next. Filer called Cowboy to the edge of the cabin and told him to make sure he had slack on the garden hose. With Cowboy acting as his ground man he started climbing a corner of the cabin where logs overlapped in a locking pattern. At the top of the wall he reached over the eave of the cabin and leveraged his way onto the roof. For the next half an hour he walked the roof ridge and wetted down the wood shingles until they were soaked. When he decided he'd wetted the roof as best he could Filer climbed back down the logs and handed the hose to Dave. Cowboy turned his section of the hose over to Scott.

"We're going back to Garrison. We've got to work tomorrow," Filer told Dave.

"That's okay. We'll stay until the fire is out. I heard the county fire fighters are on the job. If the fire gets too close and we can't handle it; Shane told me to hire more men to protect the cabin."

Two days later the forest fire was put out. Only a few sparks had reached the power line. One of the poles had been scorched, but not enough to need replacing.

CHAPTER 77

Mortimer 'Boner Man' Nelson drove a rented van on the road to Deer Lodge. Mortimer's two henchmen, Stokes and Randy, listened as he explained his plan to abduct and extort Rip-It-Up. It would happen the next night. Mortimer had high hopes he would have Rip-It-Up's thirty thousand by the weekend; and he was already trying to figure out how to stiff Leslie. "I'm doing all the work. Why should I split the money with that bitch?"

Once they arrived in Deer Lodge Mortimer led Stokes and Randy to the Broken Arrow. He took his time showing them the layout of the Arrow. Then with a little time on their hands they had dinner and settled in to wait until closing time.

CHAPTER 78

Shane and Ferra had arrived in Deer Lodge about the same time as Mortimer and his crew. Dave, Shane's General Contractor, was waiting at Shane's cabin to turn the keys over to him.

"Everything is ready. You're hooked up to the local power company and you have a telephone line ready to go."

Shane accepted the keys and Dave left the two to wander through the cabin on their own.

Shane and Ferra walked through the three thousand square foot cabin admiring the craftsmanship that had gone into completing the cabin. It wasn't in the same class as his home in Malibu, but it would do as a get-away. After unpacking their suitcases Shane called Ozzie and confirmed their plans to have a celebratory dinner at the Fireplace Inn. Shane figured they would have plenty of time to settle into the cabin.

It took them an hour to get ready to meet Ozzie and Trina at the restaurant and then they were on their way.

Despite her arguments for enjoying life in Hollywood, Ferra was happy to be with Shane and was impressed with his cabin. And to go to this dinner party she hadn't had to go shopping for a killer dress. She dressed in casual clothes that wouldn't be out of place in Deer Lodge.

Chapter 79

While Shane and his party enjoyed a late dinner at the Fireplace Inn, Rip-It-Up and his band were playing their last set at the Arrow. The crowd asked for one more and Harold looked at Nancy, the night manager. She nodded yes and Rip-It-Up followed the bartender's last call for alcohol with an energetic *Proud Mary*. After the encore, he led his band mates off the stage into the back room. They stashed their instruments in the small performers' dressing room and left out the back door. Rip-It-Up usually exited last after checking out with the manager.

When Rip-It-Up finished with Nancy he walked out the back door expecting to meet Cherie. Cherie had been in the bar sitting at a front table with her gal pals. At closing time Cherie went to the bathroom for a quick touch up to her make-up, so instead of Cherie three thugs wearing biker gear met Harold behind the bar and shoved him into a van.

Harold landed heavily on the van floor. It knocked the wind out of him and he didn't have a chance to call for help before the van's sliding door slammed shut. When he got his breath back his hands were tied behind his back. He didn't need to think about why he was grabbed-it had to be about the money.

Stokes reported to Mortimer, "He's tied up."

'Boner Man' yelled over his shoulder, "What are you waiting for? Ask him where he put the money."

"Okay man, we want the hold out money. Where is it?" Stokes questioned Harold.

Rip-It-Up didn't say anything and gave Stokes a hard stare.

"Start talking," Stokes threatened.

"What the hell," Rip-It-Up replied, "who told you I've got hold out money?"

"Don't try to B.S. us man. Your ex knows you've got thirty thousand dollars. We know you've got it here somewhere," Mortimer said glancing in the rear view mirror. Just give us the money and we'll let you go."

"Well, I don't have the money," Rip-It-Up said.

Randy looked at Mortimer and Mortimer nodded yes. Randy braced himself by widening his stance on the van floor and threw a punch knocking Rip-It-Up's head sideways.

Rip-It-Up retreated mentally and tried to think. If he told these thugs 'Mad Dog' had his money belt, they would go after him.

"Come on man," Randy screamed. He was the drunkest and most violent of the three kidnappers.

Randy pushed Stokes out of the way and smashed his fist into Rip-It-Up's face again. Harold's eye swelled shut and he bled from a cut where Randy's fist had pinched flesh against his facial bones.

"Wait a minute," Rip-It-Up pleaded.

Randy pulled his fist back for another swing and Rip-It-Up said, "Okay, okay. I'll take you to the money. But you won't be able to get it. I can't get it either." Rip-It-Up improvised wildly.

"What do you mean?" Stokes questioned the injured musician.

"The money is in a safe at Shane McLane, the movie star's cabin."

"Who's Shane McLane?" Mortimer yelled from the front seat.

"You know, Shane McLane, *Kill or be Killed*; he's got a new cabin in the mountains behind Deer Lodge. He's a friend I met in L.A., and he offered to let me keep my money in his safe."

Rip-It-Up licked blood from a split lip, waiting for his captors to decide what to do.

Randy put a hand on the van's wall and waited for Mortimer to give him instructions. Whether he had to beat on Rip-It-Up or not, made no difference to him.

"Where is this cabin?" Mortimer demanded.

"Northwest of town, take a left hand turn off of I-90 into the national forest," Rip-It-Up mumbled through damaged lips.

Stokes left Randy sitting on the van's floor guarding Harold and climbed into the van's passenger seat.

"How are we going to get into the safe?" Stokes asked Mortimer.

"We'll figure that out when we get there," Mortimer said.

CHAPTER 80

Ferra decided she liked Shane's new friends. True to his beliefs Ozzie and Trina were real people and they were all having an interesting dinner at the Fireplace Inn. They had finished the meal plus wine and now they were drinking coffee before leaving the restaurant.

Ozzie asked Shane if they wanted to have a drink or two at his R.V. before they drove out to his new cabin. Shane explained they didn't really have the cabin stocked for entertaining yet and they would be happy to take him up on his invitation.

Shane and Ferra followed Ozzie and Trina to their R.V. Once they were there they gathered in the R.V.'s small living room to drink scotches for Shane and Ozzie and white wine for Ferra and Trina. The conversation turned to country living.

"I guess I didn't really consider that I'd be living a different life style up here. I just wanted to get away from the crowds of people in L.A. Now that I'm here, the mountains with the pine trees and creeks are growing on me," Shane explained.

"For some a little place like Deer Lodge; and even a bigger city like Missoula are lacking in civilization," Ozzie offered his opinion. "If you've worked in isolated communities for most of your career, living closer to medical services, museums, and even movie theaters can be a good thing."

"See Shane even real people realize there can be some advantages in big city living," Ferra said.

The after dinner party continued while the members of the party debated the pros and cons of country living.

CHAPTER 81

Filer relaxed into his easy chair, and picked up Girlfriend so he could pet her for a minute before he went to bed. Girlfriend curled up in his lap and started purring. She had settled in with Filer for the long haul, and he figured she had won the cat equivalent of a million dollar lottery.

With the McLane job done Filer could get a few hours extra sleep. Maybe he was getting old, "Hell, for sure he was getting old. He needed his sleep to be able to get up and go to work in the morning. It was times like this he missed distribution, working out of a bucket lift and going home at night." As Girlfriend purred on his lap Filer wondered how much longer he could keep up with the younger guys like Cowboy. He'd made a career change once; maybe it was time for another change. "What could he do besides line work?" When he'd decided to try line work he'd been looking for more money; but he also wanted the excitement. Now his interests were in other directions; not money, definitely less excitement, and less hard work. With these thoughts in mind, Filer dozed off in his easy chair.

CHAPTER 82

Rip-It-Up gave final directions to Mortimer. Mortimer turned onto the dirt road leading to Shane McLane's cabin. Even in his extreme circumstances Harold couldn't help taking pride in the power line beside the dirt road. By telling the lie about his money being in Shane's safe he'd given himself a little extra time to think of his next move. He was thinking, but no next moves came to mind. Of course that excluded the Calvary arriving just in the nick of time. In his case that would be the local police force. There was the thought that maybe he could get word to the police; then he thought that wasn't likely.

Mortimer started thinking out loud, "If Rip-It-Up's money was in a safe, how would they get it? If the safe was one of those cheap home safes they could probably drop it on the floor and it would pop open. If it was a commercial job that would be another story."

Stokes sat in the passenger seat and didn't seem to be thinking anything at all. That was alright in Mortimer's view; he preferred to do the thinking for his crew.

Mortimer was somewhat startled pulling up in front of the two story log mansion Rip-It-Up had called a cabin.

"Here we are boys. Get him on his feet and let's get inside," Mortimer said, shutting off the engine and exiting the van.

Stokes got out the passenger side and pulled the van's sliding door open. With Randy on one side and Stokes on the other they pulled and dragged Rip-It-Up from the van.

"How do we get in?" Mortimer questioned their captive.

"The key is in the generator shed behind the cabin."

"Stokes, you and Randy take him to the shed and get the key, I'll wait here," Mortimer said.

"There better be a key back there," Randy threatened Rip-It-Up, "I'd love to have a chance to beat on you a little more."

"What if Ozzie moved the key or put it in his pocket to keep us from having another party," Harold thought; and for the first time Rip-It-Up was well and truly frightened as to what could happen to him at the hands of Mortimer's thugs. Then Randy found the key hung on a nail and started shoving him back to the front of the cabin.

Once everyone was inside the cabin, Mortimer directed his attention to Rip-It-Up, "Okay, where is the safe?"

"It's behind that picture of the cowboy on the wall."

"You didn't say it was a wall safe."

"You didn't ask me."

"Well, I guess we don't drop it on the floor," Stokes said sarcastically.

Mortimer gave Stokes a disgusted look.

"Our only choice is to get someone here with the combination," Mortimer said.

"Sounds good to me," Randy said. "You don't know the combination do you?" Randy asked Rip-It-Up.

"You're joking, why would I know the combination?"

Randy smacked Rip-It-Up on the back of the head.

"Well, I bet you do know who knows it, smart guy."

Mortimer heard the conversation, and said, "Good point Randy. You just earned your share."

Mortimer said, "Guitar man we need someone here who can open the safe. That means you're going to get the movie star out here to get the money for you."

"In the meantime let's have a drink," Stokes said. He opened a bottle of beer from the bar and took a swallow.

Mortimer picked up the telephone and got a dial tone.

"Come here guitar man," he commanded Rip-It-Up. "Make a call and get the big star here to open the safe."

"How am I supposed to do that? If he was in Deer Lodge he'd be here in his cabin."

"I don't care how you do it. Make a call; otherwise I'll let Randy convince you."

Randy grabbed Rip-It-Up and pulled him to the phone. Rip-It-Up took the phone. He thought for a minute. If he called Filer he could kiss his money good-bye. He didn't know how he could contact Shane. His only option was to call Ozzie. He dialed Ozzie's number and listened while the phone rang.

CHAPTER 83

Back at the Broken Arrow, when Rip-It-Up didn't meet Cherie after he left the stage, she found the night manager. The two women stood in front of the u-shaped bar.

"Where is my Harold?" Cherie asked Nancy.

"He left the bar after his last set. What he does then is none of my business," Nancy replied with an attitude.

"No need to get angry Cher," Cherie said, observing Nancy's emotional response. Then she said, "I believe you like my Harold. You must know he is my man."

"You don't know anything, you crazy biker bitch," left Nancy's lips before she had a chance to think it over.

"Now who's the nasty bitch," Cherie thought and then said, "That's enough," her own voice filling with anger.

"It won't be enough until you get the hell out of my bar. If you don't get out now I'll call the police and they'll drag you out."

"You shouldn't speak like that, woman," Cherie replied. "I think we both want the same thing-to see Harold."

At this point Nancy calmed down. "Look, I don't know what happened to Harold. Maybe he found someone else to party with. He's a free man." Nancy saw a certain look develop on Cherie's face, so she said, "Sorry. I guess I'm a little jealous."

"Ca va, mon amis," Cherie reverted to French when she got excited. Just then the cleaning man came into the bar.

Both women looked in the man's direction. Nancy called him over.

"Clarence, did you see Rip-It-Up after he finished playing?" Nancy questioned the man.

"I was emptying the trash when two men pushed him into a van." Somewhat apologetically Clarence added, "It wasn't my business ma'am."

"That's fine, Clarence. You can finish cleaning up now."

Now Nancy and Cherie were both concerned for Rip-It-Up.

"How do we find Harold?" Nancy asked Cherie.

"With my Harold there is no way to know where he could be," Cherie answered.

CHAPTER 84

'Boner Man' listened as Rip-It-Up dialed Ozzie's number. Rip-It-Up hoped Ozzie could buy him time while he tried to think of a way out of his current dilemma.

In Deer Lodge Ozzie excused himself while he answered the telephone. When he picked up the phone he heard Rip-It-Up's panicky voice on the other end of the connection.

"Ozzie, I got a bit of a problem," Rip-It-Up started explaining. "You have to get Shane to come out to his cabin." Harold had to ask for Shane even though he didn't know if Shane was in town.

"What's that?" Ozzie asked.

"I need Shane McLane to get into his safe," Harold said so Mortimer could hear, "and give me my money." Rip-It-Up hoped Ozzie would guess what was happening.

"What the hell?" Ozzie exclaimed.

"I need my money. You have to get McLane out here to open his safe."

"Okay, I get it," Ozzie said, "I'll get there as soon as I can." Ozzie knew Rip-It-Up had given his money belt to Filer, but he decided he'd go along with Rip-It-Up. "It might take a while to get McLane there. I don't know where he is." Ozzie went along with Harold's story even though Shane was sitting with Ferra on his couch.

"Thanks Ozzie," Rip-It-Up said.

Mortimer grabbed the phone from him and said, "No cops, and you'd better get that movie star fairy out here before I lose patience and give the guitar man to my boys. They're real anxious to see if he can play the guitar with broken fingers."

"I hear you," Ozzie said, "I'll get him there as soon as I can, and no cops."

Mortimer hung up the phone and Stokes pushed Rip-It-Up into a chair.

Ozzie clicked the phone dead and dialed Filer's number. He waited while it rang a few times and then Filer picked up. "Filer, this is Ozzie. We've got a problem."

For a moment Filer had an experience of Déjà vu. This conversation brought him the thought of Clayton Wilson waking him out of deep sleep with the same words Ozzie had just used; and then leading him half awake into some situation he'd sooner not have been in.

"Are you there 'Mad Dog'?"

"I'm here. What's the problem and why is it my problem?"

"Rip-It-Up is being held by some guys that want his money. They have him at Shane's cabin. He told them his emergency stash is in Shane's safe."

"Damn it. How did they find out he had the money?"

"It has to be Leslie behind this. Rip-It-Up said she'd do almost anything to get her hands on the money."

"Are you ready for this? He wants me to bring Shane to his cabin. Actually this isn't a problem because McLane and his girlfriend are sitting here with Trina and me."

Filer listened patiently. "We think the best idea is for you to come with us and give them the money belt, get Rip-It-Up back, and then call the police to get Harold's money back. That's why I called you. We want you to go with us and turn the money belt over to the kidnappers."

Filer petted Girlfriend when she landed on his lap while he listened to Ozzie.

"Rip-It-Up isn't going to be happy to lose that money. That's why he gave it to me," Filer said. "Why don't we just call the sheriff and let him handle the situation?" Filer wanted to know.

"One of the kidnappers said if they see or hear the police they will break his fingers or worse. The police can't get in quick enough to save his fingers. These guys are thugs and I think they will keep their word about doing something to Rip-It-Up.

"Okay, give me fifteen minutes and I'll drive to your place. We can go out to the cabin together."

CHAPTER 85

After Nancy called the police, Cherie sat at the bar while Nancy finished her closing chores. Her thoughts were on Harold. How could she find him? He might need her help. If he was forced into a van it probably had something to do with that bitch Leslie. Too bad Leslie was in Portland. She could make Leslie tell her who had taken Harold. Now her best chance for more information could be calls to Harold's friends in Deer Lodge.

"May I use your phone?" Cherie asked Nancy.

"As long as the calls are local; no calls to Canada," Nancy started to regain an attitude.

Cherie ignored the catty remark and dialed Ozzie Harper's number. Harold had introduced her to Ozzie and Trina during an earlier trip to Deer Lodge.

"Hello," Trina answered the phone.

"This is Cherie Bon Temp. Harold is missing. Some men pushed him into a van behind the Broken Arrow. Now he's gone," Cherie finished in a forlorn tone. I need to speak to Ozzie."

"Wait a minute," Trina said.

Cherie heard Trina yell for Ozzie to come to the phone.

Cherie paced back and forth in the bar as far as she could with the phone in her hand.

Ozzie took the phone from Trina and listened to Cherie. Then he explained what had happened to Harold. "Rip-It-Up has been kidnapped. The kidnappers want his hold out stash."

"I knew it. It's that bitch Leslie. She wants to hurt Harold. She doesn't need the money," Cherie let her feelings go, and then she calmed down. "Where have they taken Harold?"

"It won't do you any good to know where he's at. They're threatening to torture Harold if they don't get the money." Ozzie thought for a minute and then said, "Why don't you come to my place." It would be better if he could keep an eye on Cherie rather than leaving her as a loose cannon. Ozzie gave Cherie directions for getting to his R.V.

"I'll be there in ten minutes," Cherie said and hung up the bar phone. Once she was off the phone she told Nancy what Ozzie had told her and then said, "You stay here and tell the police what you know when they get here. I'm going to try and help get Harold away from kidnappers.

"What?" Nancy wanted more details.

"Don't worry. You'll be most helpful to stay here Cher," Cherie reassured Nancy, and walked out of the bar.

CHAPTER 86

Twenty minutes after Rip-It-Up called Ozzie, Filer arrived at Ozzie's R.V. with the money belt and saw Shane, Ferra and Cherie sitting in the living room with Ozzie and Trina.

Ozzie asked Filer if he could see the money belt.

"It's okay. If anyone is going to give it to the kidnappers it's going to be me," Filer said.

Despite his leading man roles Shane had to ask, "What do we do now?"

"Well," Ozzie said, "we all get in your new Blazer and drive out to the cabin." Then he added, "I think the ladies should stay here," and he looked at Trina to emphasis his point.

"Right," Shane agreed squeezing Ferra's hand.

"Trina and Ferra didn't object, but Cherie said, "It's my Harold they have and I won't stay here. I have to go with you." She put on a determined expression to go with her declaration.

Ozzie glanced at the men and they didn't disagree.

"Okay then; do we go in with or without guns?"

"I don't have a gun," Shane was ashamed to admit. "All of my guns are at the cabin."

Filer said, "I'm taking my .357. Better to have it and not need it than to need it and not have it."

"Ozzie," Trina started to caution her husband.

"I've got a .38 and you're right. If they see we've got some protection it will be better for us."

"What about me?" Shane asked, "Do you have an extra pistol for me?"

"Trina honey, would you give him that cute little piece you carry in your purse?" Ozzie asked Trina.

Trina went to their bedroom where she kept her purse and returned with a Beretta. "Please be careful out there, all of you. I want my husband and my gun back."

Cherie didn't say anything about being armed so she wasn't asked if she wanted a gun.

"I guess we're ready then," Ozzie said and led the group of rescuers out of the R.V. to Shane's Blazer.

On the road, Ozzie said, "I don't know how many men are at the cabin, so we'll just have to wait and see what we're up against. But I think our best bet is to show them we can take care of ourselves, and that they should turn Rip-It-Up over to us before we give them the money belt."

No one disagreed with Ozzie's plan.

CHAPTER 87

At Shane McLane's cabin Mortimer directed his crew to tie Rip-It-Up to one of the wooden kitchen chairs. Mortimer figured with Rip-It-Up tied up he would be one less person to worry about when the movie star arrived to open the wall safe.

With Rip-It-Up secured to the kitchen chair, Stokes and Randy decided they were free to drink more of Shane's liquor. Mortimer didn't drink, but he didn't try stopping the other two from drinking.

"How much is our share?" Stokes wanted to know.

"Wait until we actually have the money to split," Mortimer said.

"Well then, theoretically, how much is our share?" Stokes tried another approach. "You said the bitch wouldn't get a nickel. How much is my share?" Stokes started to get annoying.

Randy listened closely to the exchange between Mortimer and Stokes.

"Slow down on the booze Stokes. You still have to earn whatever share you get. Now shut your yap about the money."

There was silence in the cabin for five minutes, than Randy asked, "Are they coming? Maybe they called the cops, and the cops are on the way."

"Thanks for your input Randy. I'll keep my eyes open and if we get surrounded by the cops you'll be the first to know," Mortimer said.

CHAPTER 88

Shane drove his Blazer along the gravel road beside his private power line. Usually on a drive like this, with this many people in the Blazer, there would be talking and laughter. On this ride all the passengers were keeping to themselves. All of their thoughts were focused on rescuing Rip-It-Up Roberts from the kidnappers. Each mile raised tension in the SUV, until finally Shane's cabin appeared in the forest clearing ahead.

"Here we are," Shane announced. "What do we do now?"

Ozzie took charge of the situation. "Filer has the money belt, but when we get inside I'll do the talking. Everyone wear your pistols where the kidnappers can see them. We don't know if we out number them so we put on a real show of strength. Then we ask them to release Roberts before we turn over the money belt. Does that sound right to you Filer?"

Filer put the money belt over his shoulder like a bandoleer and nodded his head yes.

"Now Shane, you and Cherie come in behind Filer and me and cover us." Cherie surprised them by pulling a six shooter at least as big as Filer's .357 out of her shoulder bag.

"Whoa there," Ozzie said, "you sure you know how to use that piece?"

"Oui," Cherie answered in her excited French. "Of course, I'm from the wild west in Canada."

"Anyway," Ozzie went on, "you and Shane will be covering Filer and me and when we get inside, make sure you let the bad guys see your guns."

CHAPTER 89

In the cabin, Mortimer heard gravel crunching as Shane's Blazer arrived. He looked at his crew and wondered about his choice in bad men. They were looking at him with puzzled expressions. "Was this the best he could expect?"

"Okay you guys, it's time," Mortimer said to get their undivided attention. He had Stokes check Rip-It-Up to see if he was still tied up tight.

"He's not going anywhere," Stokes reported.

"You guys keep your eyes open. Once the safe's open and we get the money we lock everyone in the basement; and then we're out of here."

Bloody Randy objected, "I don't know man, I mean maybe we should just waste 'em. They'll have seen us. They could identify us."

"Look Randy, we're a repo team, not murderers."

Randy didn't look happy, but he said, "Whatever you say man."

Stokes looked at Mortimer as if he agreed with Randy.

Mortimer said, "What? Are you crazy? Do you want to end up on death row? We're not going to kill anyone."

A pounding on the door brought their conversation to an end.

Mortimer pulled the gun from his front waistband. "Get the door Stokes," he commanded.

Stokes opened the door and was forced back by Ozzie and Filer coming through the door together.

"What the hell?" Stokes exclaimed as he fell back beside Mortimer.

"We're here to get Rip-It-Up," Ozzie said with his gun in hand. The room fell silent when Shane and Cherie came in behind Ozzie and Filer.

"We have the money with us," Ozzie said, and then looked around the room counting the number of men holding Rip-It-Up. It didn't take long for him to figure that the rescuers outnumbered and out gunned the kidnappers. "But first we have to have a talk." He looked at the rescuers, and then went on, "It looks to me like we outnumber and out gun you boys." Ozzie paused to let his point sink in.

Mortimer took another look at the rescuers. He looked at Stokes, and Stokes gave him a puzzled stare in return. Next 'Boner Man' looked at Randy. Randy maintained his mean 'break a bone' expression. Then, as if Mortimer suddenly recognized the truth of Ozzie's statement, he returned to looking at Ozzie with a facial expression mixing threat and confusion.

"Give us Rip-It-Up and you get the money. All we want is to trade Rip-It-Up for the money," Ozzie exclaimed, and looked at Filer.

Filer touched the money belt slung over his shoulder.

Mortimer seemed to still be taking in what Ozzie said about the rescuers outnumbering and out gunning his crew. His confused expression overtook the threatening expression when he asked, "What about the safe?"

"The money wasn't in the safe," Rip-It-Up yelled from the kitchen. "I told you that because I didn't want them to give you the money." Harold continued yelling-at Filer, "Way to go Buddy. I thought my money was safe with you. You know that's all the money I have in the world."

Mortimer recovered from his confused state and aimed his gun at Ozzie, "Give us the money and the guitar man is yours."

Ozzie said, "Keep fooling around with that pistol and something bad is going to happen."

'Boner Man' responded by telling Randy to point his gun at Harold's head. Then he said, "All we want is the money. Give us the money belt and we'll clear out of here." To make matters clear he explained, "First you hand over the money belt, then we go out the door and Roberts is yours."

Ozzie looked at the rescuers and they all nodded in agreement. He signaled their approval of his plan to Mortimer.

Mortimer yelled at Randy, "Cut the guitar man loose and stand him up."

Randy did as instructed.

"Walk him over here," Mortimer said. "Now you guys go over by the fireplace," Mortimer motioned at Ozzie's group with his gun.

"You, with the beard," Mortimer began, "hand me the money belt."

Filer broke out of the group and handed Mortimer the bulky money belt and retreated to the group at the fireplace.

Now the rescuers waited for Mortimer to live-up to his part of the deal.

As the three bad guys backed out of the room towards the door holding Harold as a shield, a dangerous stand off still existed in the cabin. With the door at his back, Mortimer directed Stokes, "Stokes keep your gun on them."

Hostile, apprehensive stares flashed back and forth between the two groups.

Shane clued in on the tense situation and remembered how cowboys in the western movies hovered a hand over their holstered pistols, meeting the steely gaze of their opponents with steely gazes of their own. Unconsciously his hand moved to hover above the Beretta in his waistband. The other rescuers all moved their hands to the weapons tucked into their waistbands. The situation could still turn into a gun battle.

While Stokes kept his gun on the group, and Randy had his gun pointed at Rip-It-Up's head, Mortimer stopped at the door, opened the first pocket in the money belt and checked the contents. When he had counted a thousand dollars worth of tens and twenties he opened the third pocket and counted a second thousand. Filer watched Mortimer intently as he finished counting the third pocket full of bills.

"Stokes get out the door and start the van," Mortimer said. "Randy, you get in front of me and when I get out the door, you back out and push the guitar man back into the cabin."

Randy protested, "I thought we were going to lock them in the basement."

'Boner Man' sighed in exasperation, "Hadn't Randy heard the bit about being outnumbered and out gunned."

"Change of plans man. We leave them with the guitar man and they let us go," he said and looked past Randy at Ozzie.

"That's right. No need to complicate things. Give us Rip-It-Up and you can drive away."

Mortimer didn't wait for Randy to register his approval or disapproval. He heard Stokes start the van and stepped out the door. Randy backed out the door and at the last minute shoved Rip-It-Up into the cabin.

With all of the bad guys out of the cabin, Cherie ran to Rip-It-Up and pulled him into her arms.

"I'll be damned," Shane said, "so that's how it works in real life. I thought I'd shit my pants when we faced off with those guys."

"Are you crazy? You just gave away my hold out money," Rip-It-Up yelled at Filer.

Filer smiled and said, "How much is it worth to you not to be dead? It just cost you fifteen thousand dollars to get them out of here. That's all the money that was in the money belt. Now if it's okay with you we had better make a plan to get out of here before they decide to count all of those one dollar bills I put in the money belt to fill the rest of the pockets."

Harold continued to rant, "Where's the rest of my money?"

"I'll tell you all about that when we get back to Deer Lodge. Filer looked at Ozzie and said, "We should call the Deer Lodge police department and tell them what happened."

Filer didn't know Nancy had told the police Harold had been kidnapped, and that Trina had also called and told them they should investigate a break in at the famous movie star's cabin.

CHAPTER 90

The Deer Lodge police chief responded to the burglary call concerning the newly built Shane McLane cabin. He called in all of his deputies and went to the scene with lights flashing and sirens wailing. On top of a need to get to the bottom of the emergency call, he had a curiosity to see the movie star's getaway place in the woods.

Halfway up the private road leading to the cabin, Chief of Police Sloan saw a van coming towards his patrol car and it didn't look like it was going to stop. Over his car phone he directed the cruisers following him to form a road block. Once the occupants of the van saw the cruisers blocking the road ahead they stopped and ran for the woods.

The chief of police said to the deputy beside him, "This is going to be too easy. How far do you think those guys are going to make it before they give up?"

The deputy responded, "Probably after they get whacked in the face with the heavy brush a few times."

"Okay, take some men and run them down. I'll go up to the cabin and see what's going on there."

At the end of the forest road, Chief of Police Sloan parked his vehicle and directed his men toward the cabin, all with guns drawn, moving forward in a controlled manner.

Inside the cabin Ozzie, Filer, and Cherie had given their pistols to Shane so he could hide them when they heard the police sirens. Now they were waiting with Rip-It-Up in the living room. When they heard a banging on the front door Shane got up and let the chief of police and his deputies in. The chief demanded, "Hands up," and then had his deputies verify all of their identities. When he had established that Shane was the owner of the cabin and the people gathered around him were his guests he relaxed, and after instructing his men to holster their weapons he also put his gun away.

Back in Deer Lodge the chief interviewed kidnappers and rescuers. Mortimer and his crew told a tale of how Harold had ripped off his former wife. According to him, he'd been hired to repossess the money. They hadn't done anything wrong.

Next the chief interviewed Rip-It-Up and discovered he had taken the money out of his account to stop his ex from stealing it. It was a question of law whether or not Leslie was entitled to any part of the thirty thousand, but first she would have to answer to charges of instigating a kidnapping.

After interviewing Ozzie and Filer the chief started putting the pieces together. As he saw it, their rescue operation was outside the law. Instead of confronting a group of armed men they should have come to him. Acting as vigilantes was against the law.

In the end the real crime had been planning to kidnap Rip-It-Up by Leslie, and her hiring of thugs to carry out her scheme. Why hadn't she hired a lawyer like a sane person?

Mortimer and his crew were charged with armed assault and kidnapping. Now it was up to a judge to get life back to normal in Deer Lodge.

Just when the chief thought he had a handle on the situation a high powered lawyer showed up to represent Shane and the rest of the rescuers. Shane had used his phone call to contact his agent who then hired the most expensive lawyer in Deer Lodge. After hearing their story the lawyer assured them they hadn't done anything wrong, and he convinced the chief to release the rescuers.

Mortimer, Stokes and Randy weren't so lucky. They ended up arrested and put in jail waiting for trial. The Deer Lodge chief of police contacted the Portland police department and told them about Leslie Roberts part in planning the kidnapping of Harold Roberts.

CHAPTER 91

After an uncomfortable night in jail, Filer got in his truck at Ozzie's place and drove back to his trailer. He'd only been there minutes when he heard a knocking at his door. Harold Roberts looked about as angry as Filer had ever seen him when he opened the door and invited him into his trailer.

After Rip-It-Up stopped yelling, Filer told him to calm down.

"You got your money belt back from the chief of police, didn't you?"

"Yeah, but it was light fifteen thousand dollars."

"Your belt only had fifteen thousand dollars in it because I invested fifteen thousand."

"You did what?"

"I invested part of your hold out stash. Now tell me you've given up loan sharking since the old days."

Rip-It-Up assumed a twisted, uncomfortable expression and said, "I might loan out a few bucks here and there."

"That's what I thought. The way I remember it, you loaned out money to losers who had a hot tip on a sure thing."

"That's not fair. I loaned money to guys who were going to lose their only way of getting to work; and other good causes."

"Stop, you're breaking my heart."

"I suppose you invested my money in an orphanage."

"Better than that; come with me to Deer Lodge and I'll show you your investment."

Rip-It-Up and Filer got into Filer's truck. They rode to Deer Lodge in silence. In Deer Lodge, Filer parallel parked in front of a main street shop.

"What are we doing here?" Rip-It-Up wanted to know.

Before Filer took Rip-It-Up into the shop he stopped outside so Rip-It-Up could read the name of the shop. A fancy lettering job proclaimed *Glitter and Glam for all your Beauty needs.*

"Do you think I need a facial or something?"

"Step inside amigo," Filer said with a smile and held the door open.

Rip-It-Up stepped through the open glass door into the beauty salon. The shop's interior was filled with hair and beauty treatment stations on one side, and a line of hair dryers on the other. Several startled women looked at Rip-It-Up and Filer when the shop door closed behind them.

A good looking woman by the cash register spoke, "Well, well 'Mad Dog', did you come in for a facial, or to get your beard trimmed?"

Filer smiled, "Neither one Shirley, I have your business partner here to meet you."

Glitter and Rip-It-Up looked at one another and then at Filer.

Glitter asked one of the beauticians who was tidying up her station to take over for her, and motioned the two men to follow her into the back room. Once inside her office Glitter sat at her desk and nodded for Filer and Rip-It-Up to sit in the red plastic seats facing her.

Rip-It-Up took a closer look at Glitter, "Hey, I recognize you from Fred's. You're one of the strippers."

"I was one of the strippers, but not anymore," Glitter replied, "I'm a small business owner now! And I guess I owe part of my good fortune to you, according to what Filer told me."

"He hasn't explained it to me yet."

Glitter and Rip-It-Up turned to hear Filer's explanation.

"After you gave me your money belt, Glitter came to see me with a little problem. She told me she needed a loan until she got her small business loan. I would have helped her, but I didn't have the money. Then I got to thinking about a safe place to put your emergency stash. The rest is history. Now you have a choice. You'll get all your money back as soon as Shirley gets her small business loan money."

Rip-It-Up gave Filer a doubtful look.

"Don't worry, buddy, the loan is approved and Shirley should be getting the money real soon." Filer stopped speaking to take a breath. "As Shirley explained it to me, you have two choices: you can get your money back with interest, or you can become her business partner and take a share of the profits on a monthly basis."

Rip-It-Up looked like he needed a little time to make up his mind.

"Take your time Rip-It-Up. Either way you're going to get your money back with a little extra," Shirley promised. "Let me know when you make up your mind. Now gentlemen I've got a beauty shop to run."

Filer used Shirley's phone to call Highline Electric and take a personal day.

After Filer's call, Glitter got up from her desk and showed Filer and Rip-It-Up out the office door.

In the shop three blue haired ladies smiled at Filer and Rip-It-Up, and the beauticians styling their hair gave Filer an especially big smile.

On Main Street, outside the shop, Rip-It-Up stopped Filer and held out his hand. "You did good buddy. I knew you'd take good care of my money. Stop by the Arrow and I'll buy you dinner and drinks."

Chapter 92

Filer drove Rip-It-Up back to his trailer. Rip-It-Up shook Filer's hand again and left the trailer court. Abbey called just as Filer walked in the door. For the next hour, with Girlfriend curled on the couch next to him, he told her about his latest adventure. It definitely wasn't the story he would tell in a bar over a pitcher of beer, but he hit the high spots.

"Filer, your story sounds like the kind of thing Clayton used to get you into. Are you alright?"

"I'm fine. Everyone is fine and the bad guys are in jail. Leslie will be arrested by the police in Portland. And I have another good story to tell."

"When can you come home?"

"I'll be home next weekend."

CHAPTER 93

When the cold winds of winter prompted Highline Electric to shut down work on the line of steel towers that would carry electricity from the heart of Montana to Washington; Filer Wilson moved his Nomad trailer back to Albany, Oregon, to its comfortable berth beside the family home.

A week after he arrived in Albany, Filer got a phone call from Ozzie.

"Hey there 'Mad Dog', how's the home life going?"

"Just relaxing Ozzie; getting use to being at home again."

"That's good 'Mad Dog'," Ozzie said.

Filer listened, waiting for Ozzie to go on.

"Didn't Rupert stay with you this summer?"

"Worst week of my life; he asked all kinds of questions. Ate my food and left messes in the kitchen and bathroom."

"Yeah, he asked me a lot of questions," Ozzie said. "Anyway Filer, it looks like he actually did finish writing the book he was talking about. He called it *The Copper Thieves*, and you're in it big time."

Ozzie couldn't see the amazed look on Filer's face when he asked, "Have you read it, Ozzie?"

"He sent me a copy. It's pretty good. I'm surprised you didn't get a copy."

"I don't remember giving him my address in Albany."

Ozzie's voice seemed even more excited than before, "That's not all the news, 'Mad Dog'."

"This just keeps getting better," Filer thought.

"You still there, 'Mad Dog'?"

"I'm still here."

"Rupert gave a copy of his book to Rip-It-Up and asked him to give it to Shane McLane. Shane read the book and liked it a lot. Now listen to this 'Mad Dog'."

Filer didn't know what to think as he waited for Ozzie to go on.

Ozzie continued, "Shane gave the book to a producer he knows, and the producer liked the book enough that he is putting up money to make the book into a movie."

"Holy shit," Filer exclaimed.

"There's more," Ozzie said, "Shane called me and told me to tell you he wants you in Hollywood to be a technical advisor, and his stunt man. Shane's going to play you."

"Say that again Ozzie."

"That's right, Buddy. You're going to be in a movie."

ABOUT THE AUTHOR

Why do I write? Asking why I write is like asking extreme athletes why they participate in their sports. They like the way their bodies respond to the activity. Fitness is a secondary benefit. Writers write because writing exercises the mind and the end result of words on a page having a pattern and a rhythm satisfies the human necessity for pleasing and effective communication.

How am I qualified to write what I'm writing and what I've written? If you are an aspiring writer, you've probably heard the advice-"write what you know." I've had a lucky life. My uncle once said my nickname should be Lucky. I agree with him, just not for his reasons. Having served in the Navy during the Vietnam War, I attended Idaho State University on the G.I. Bill. Later, while working as a Library Associate for the Chicago Public Library, I earned a Master's Degree in Library Science paid for by the City of Chicago. The City of Chicago built a new central library and needed more librarians. The cheapest and best way to get more librarians was to encourage Library Associates to become Librarians by paying for them to go to Library School. To earn my M.L.S., I worked full time at the library and attended Library School part time for two years. What is my point? I've been lucky to be able to take advantage of various opportunities that have come to me by working to make the most of them. On the other hand, I've had a lot of experiences in my life because I didn't have a particular ambition or an overall plan for my life from an early age. This means that I've filled the inbetweens with a lot of different experiences which increased my "what you know" factor. Walt Disney World employee, ground man for an electrical construction company, Peace Corps Volunteer, Community Action agent, Substitute Teacher , plus all of the various day labor jobs I've done fill out my "what you know" list.

What is my purpose or motive for writing? Retirement has presented me with another lucky opportunity. I have the daily opportunities to work on my property and to write the books I've always told myself I could write if I had the time. I write because I like the way I can put words on the page for the same reason I like to landscape and care for my property. If you drive by and like the way my lawn looks that is a plus. If readers like what I've written and tell me they like what I've written for whatever reasons-this is also a plus.

Beginning in 2004 I've lived in Soda Springs, Idaho, closer to my family. For the last year, my brother Everett and I have been collaborating on *Mad Dog Steel Time*. *Mad Dog Steel Time* is a novel based on his years in Montana building steel tower transmission lines.